She drained the last of her cold coffee and watched the sun peel away the morning mist. The campus looked remarkably as it had thirty-five years earlier. There were a few changes. The new Communications building, a stone and glass behemoth, named for a beloved professor caught her eye. The Post Office, which had been the hub of campus life, had vanished. Some of the familiar buildings had been enlarged and the campus appeared more crowded and less pastoral than she remembered. Still, though, there were the green velvet hills and the whispered hush that enveloped this place on a summer's morning.

It had been so long. A lifetime really and yet, as she leaned against her car and looked out, a wave of emotion hit her hard and stole away her breath. "I've come home," she whispered, "the Prodigal Returneth...."

Her reverie was interrupted by the approach of an apparent member of the "undead." The young girl, disguised as a shadow and accessorized in chains and leather, her midnight black hair spiked with violet streaks, waved and walked toward her. The Gothic look was in stark contrast to the girl's smile that was broad and friendly and completely disarming.

"Hi. I'm Heather. Are you an alumnae?" She bubbled.

Alumna, Molly thought, but said nothing. Instead she returned the girl's smile and nodded affirmatively.

"You're not supposed to park here. There are spots reserved in the parking lot. I can ride over there with you, if you'd like."

Molly marveled at the innocence of the girl. I could be a serial killer she thought and without knowing me at all, without the slightest qualm, she would get in my car. She thought of admonishing the student, but then decided against it. It was rather refreshing that youth could still have faith in humanity and after all, Molly was not *very* dangerous.

"It's okay. I'll just leave it here. I plan to visit the chapel and then take a little walk around campus. I probably won't be that long." Molly assured her.

The smile faded from the girl's face.

"They'll ticket you," she warned.

"It won't be the first time," Molly said flatly. She didn't want Heather to think her unfriendly, so she added, in what she hoped was a warmer tone, "Really, it's okay."

Patience is foreign to the young and the girl's frustration erased the grin and replaced it with a look more in keeping with her apparel. "There's a booth where you can register, next to the parking lot," she said authoritatively.

"I'll register later. Maybe, after lunch."

The girl brightened. "There's free lunch in the Dining Hall. Would you like me to reserve a spot for you?

"Sure." Molly acquiesced.

"I need to know what class you are."

"Seventy-six." Molly answered.

"My grandfather was Class of Seventy. He says that St. Anthony had really good basketball teams then. He didn't play or anything, but he says it was really something then. You know, back in the day. Was it '76 that we went to the NEA finals?

"I don't think so." Molly replied, trying not to sound too grandparentish. There would be no dining hall lunch now. There would instead be clean, crisp linen and the serving of fine wine in crystal stemware. Perhaps several toasts to Heather's grandfather and the golden days of victorious basketball teams might be in order.

"You know, Heather, I might just eat in town. I need to run some errands in there anyway. Listen, I'm sure you've got a ton of things to do and I really just want to walk around a little, so maybe I'll see you later."

Heather was furiously texting on her phone, thumbs moving at near invisible speed. She was completely oblivious to Molly's valiant effort to escape.

"Contacting your mother ship?" Molly asked quietly.

"Heather?" It was Molly's turn to be frustrated. She cleared her throat audibly.

"Huh? Sorry. Seventy-six." Heather did not look up. "Was that the class that had the murder?"

"One of them." Molly replied knowingly and walked away.

CHAPTER I

Nancy Kiernan 　　　　　　　　**December, 1976**

Journalism 305 　　　　　　　　**Investigative Writing**

The heat broke. Rain hammered down upon the parched grass, dusty cars and open-shirted pedestrians. Flashes of lightning, deafening thunder and a relentless wind vented the full fury of the storm upon the sleepy afternoon. A small child, soaked and terrified, sought shelter on the back porch of a nearby house.

She wiped the rain from her face and peered through the screen door. She stared at the puddle of rainwater on the kitchen counter-top. She watched as the water formed a rivulet and dripped slowly and rhythmically onto the lifeless, bloody body of Louise Porter.

That summer storm occurred two decades ago. Twenty years have passed since Louise Porter's murder threw this college town into chaos. Yet, the questions surrounding Louise Porter's murder remain unanswered. Who killed her? Why was her life taken so suddenly and so brutally? Where is her killer today? These answers exist. They are here. They lie buried beneath the cloak of respectability this University so nobly wears. It is time to exhume those answers. Justice demands it, our conscience commands it and the ghost of Louise Porter cries out for it.

Those cries desecrate the sacred silence of the chapel. They haunt the darkened corridors and empty classrooms. They echo in the quiet places of this campus, in the still waking hours of the morning. Listen. You can hear them. It is time. It is time. It is time...

Molly shook her head and returned the typewritten page to the desk. If nothing else, Nancy had a flair for the dramatic. The assignment had been simple. Write an investigative piece about something relating to the University. Molly had undertaken the case of some missing cinder blocks from a campus construction site. When the blocks appeared as part of a makeshift bookcase in a friend's dorm room, Molly applied her best creative talents. She secured a promise that the ill-gotten goods would be returned at the end of the semester. Then she wrote the article, avoided names, waxed poetic wherever possible and turned in the piece. Case closed. She reasoned that it was not so much what you write as how you write it. It was symptomatic of what Nancy referred to as Molly's "B-mentality." Actually, C's were fine with Molly, but occasionally innate talent won out and unexpectedly, many might have contended undeservedly, yielded a higher grade.

Nancy, on the other hand, definitely possessed an "A+ mentality." If there had been a "best newborn" award in the nursery, Nancy Kiernan would have brought it home with her bunting. She would surely ace the Investigative Writing Course. (It wasn't necessary to solve a murder case to do so. Journalism was a tough major at St. Anthony but it was not that tough.) No, it wasn't any course requirement that set Nancy to this particular task. It was Nancy's unrelenting ambition. She had already garnered every honor the University could bestow on a Senior Journalism Major. She was President of Sigma Delta Chi, recipient of the Marcus Journalism Award and Class Valedictorian. So why was it necessary for Nancy Kiernan to delve into a murder? Molly sighed. For Nancy, it was not enough. However unlikely, it was possible, at least theoretically, that some other senior, some other year, might match Nancy's record of accomplishments. This was to be Nancy's parting shot, something that couldn't be matched. This was the one thing that couldn't be equaled.

Molly thought about Nancy. She pictured Nancy Eleanore Kiernan walking across campus, the long stride and quick gait, the little bit of swing from the hips. Nancy was startlingly alive. She was electric and the current ran close to the surface. You could feel it. She exuded raw energy.

There was something else. The way her sable hair fell automatically into soft waves, the polished teeth, the casual but expensive clothes. The enormous wealth and power of the Kiernans were manifest in Nancy. When you added Nancy's own drive and personality the result was explosive. No one doubted that Miss Nancy Kiernan would leave her mark on the world but it wouldn't necessarily be the result of the way she put words together in a sentence. It was because Nancy Kiernan was a shark, always poised and ready for attack. Her brown eyes could light with laughter or flash with anger, but behind them the control level did not change. She was in charge, moving steadily toward a goal. She had tasted blood and now she was moving instinctively and indefatigably toward the kill.

Molly had no taste for blood. She was a worrier. She weighed consequences. People were going to be hurt by Nancy's article and that hurt would remain. Perhaps Nancy would unearth some important information and perhaps she wouldn't. One thing was certain though -- she would dredge up a ton of painful memories in the process.

There was something inherently wrong with that equation. Quite frankly, it didn't balance. But then, so much about Nancy seemed out of sync. For example, her friendship with Molly or for that matter, Nancy's bond to the entire Monaghan family, was more than puzzling. Nancy could have gone anywhere during vacations, skiing at an exclusive lodge, tanning on some island with a Saint's name, but she chose instead a seat at the crowded Monaghan kitchen table and the rather noisy and chaotic atmosphere of what Molly called Monaghan Manor.

Nancy was the youngest of the Kiernans, the only daughter in a family of wealthy and politically powerful men. If her family had any closet relatives or social scars, they were not evident. Nancy never complained of aged relatives who fed tobacco to small dogs or a stray cousin who might need bail money or an aunt that refused to wear undergarments.

Four much older brothers, handsome, athletic and keenly intelligent, had already set the bar tremendously high for Nancy. Ironically, though, Molly had the distinct impression that Nancy didn't need to achieve anything. (At least, not in order to gain her family's love and respect.)

They seemed to idolize Nan. From her infancy, they had treated her with kid gloves. If any of her brothers had chosen Saint Anthony, instead of a traditional Ivy League college, there might have been an explosion worthy of a seven on the Richter scale. Molly never did quite understand why Nancy hadn't gone Ivy League. She had the smarts, the money and the pedigree. Molly asked Nancy once, how her parents had responded to her choice of colleges.

"Were they disappointed?" Molly asked tentatively.

"Why would they be *disappointed*?" There was an edge to her reply. Nancy thought Molly loved this place. Why would she suddenly characterize it was a disappointing choice?

"C'mon. You could have gone anywhere, even Harvard or Yale or some other big name, blue-blood institution of higher learning."

Nancy laughed. "My blood's not that blue, she explained. My mother's family has money and some history, DAR and all of that, but my father's grandfather was a saloon keeper, who may have been a bookie or numbers runner or something more than a little shady. My grandfather had his hand in everything – politics, business (both legitimate and slightly to the left of the law.) He found a way to get an education and he made sure his children were educated. So my father grew up with some money and a great education, but to real blue-bloods he has never been more than a slick "mick." It was important to my grandfather that his sons marry well and go to the right colleges, so they did."

Molly wasn't sure what that last part meant. She knew the Kiernans and had even spent time in their home. They were cordial and Mr. and Mrs. Kiernan certainly seemed to get along. Molly hoped that they were body and soul, can't imagine my life without you, in love with one another.

She wished that for all married couples. Yet, she knew it wasn't true for everyone. Mrs. Kiernan was quiet and social but Molly wouldn't have wanted to be the waiter who got her order wrong or the maid who broke a vase. Molly wondered now, if Nancy's parents had married for convenience, rather than love. She realized then, that she wasn't analyzing some characters in a story, but her friend's family and willed herself to stop. Molly had rules about that. It was too easy to dehumanize people. It was a pitfall for a writer. In trying to make the "on paper" characters real, it was almost natural to forget the depth and feelings of real people. In life, mistakes and injuries aren't erasable.

"He sounds like Joe Kennedy." Molly commented referring to Nancy's grandfather.

"He wouldn't have cared for that comparison. We are not Kennedyphiles" Nancy said flatly. Molly was a Kennedyphile, a Kennedy follower, a fan. Molly remembered the excitement of John Kennedy's nomination, the campaign button that changed from the printed "Vote for Kennedy in '60" to Kennedy's smiling face. (Molly's teacher had taken it away from her at school because Molly kept moving around in her seat, playing with the button. Kennedy's face, Vote for Kennedy, Kennedy's face. If she moved just the right way both images were visible. She smiled whenever she remembered that. Molly thought it was no small feat.

Her teacher was not amused.) She was directed to wear it from that point forward only before and after school. The night of Kennedy's election, Molly was allowed to stay up all nights and she celebrated the first Irish Catholic President with a holiday from school. Like all of America, she remembered John Kennedy's assassination and being glued to the television during those dark days of November. Molly had a collection of Kennedy cards, Kennedy pictures and books and a coveted autographed copy of "Profiles in Courage." She owned two records of Kennedy speeches that she played regularly. She loved to read and to listen to Kennedy words and phrases, both Jack's and Bobby's. She found them eloquent and inspirational. She was impressed with the Kennedys' penchant for quoting philosophers and writers. It seemed to Molly that they were as in love with language as she was. When Bobby Kennedy quoted Shakespeare's Romeo and Juliet at the 1964 Democratic Convention, it broke Molly's young heart and made her an early devotee of the Avon Bard. She knew some people didn't like the Kennedys but to Molly that was like not celebrating St. Patrick's Day. It was foreign and slightly suspect.

It wasn't really that surprising, though that Nancy's grandfather disliked Joe Kennedy. Nancy's family was Republican – the Calvin Coolidge, "The business of America is business" variety. They would have viewed their and the Kennedys' parallel social rise with the same dread as a genetic predisposition to alcoholism.

The Kiernans were correct. They were charming people, with a strong sense of the appropriate and Nancy definitely belonged to them. She had presence, determination and perhaps, a touch of haughtiness.

Yet, she chose Molly as a friend and she chose the Monaghans as a second family. She loved the emotional push and pull of the Monaghan Clan. She loved the dinners full of non-sequitors, uncontained laughter and instant indigestion. She loved the unconditional way the Monaghans opened their home and their hearts to her. She didn't understand it. There was no hint of reserve in the Monaghans, no emotional lines of demarcation. They were at once welcoming and overwhelming.

Almost upon meeting Molly's family, Nancy became "Our Nancy" to the Monaghans. The boys teased her mercilessly and Mrs. Monaghan chided her for working too hard. They hugged Nancy and kidded Nancy and loved Nancy and she hugged and kidded and loved them in return. The difference between Miss Nancy Kiernan, the St. Anthony student, aloof, diligent and slightly arrogant and "Our Nancy," Molly's friend, was startling. To Molly, it made sense: Quid pro quo. With Nancy, Molly could be serious. With Molly, Nancy could be fun. Both were writers, believers in the magic of words and both loved and were loved by the Monaghan family.

At first, Nancy had been surprised, almost shocked, by her instantaneous adoption by Molly's family. When she confided as much to her friend, Molly simply shook her head and explained, "It's part of the legacy. Centuries ago, the greatest rank you could receive in Ireland was Hospitaller. It meant you gave the best parties, had the most enjoyable home, that kind of thing. Strangers were welcome in your home. In addition, in ancient times, it was common practice for kings to kind of trade a child with a neighboring king, something of a lend-lease policy. The child was raised as a child of the other family and then returned to his natural parents as an adult. The thinking was you're less likely to go to war with someone who raised you. It didn't always work." Molly added. "Anyway, family is very big to the Irish, but it has always been more a matter of heart than blood."

It was typical of Molly to cite ancient tradition to explain current phenomenon. Then she had closed the discussion by smiling and saying, "On the other hand, perhaps my mother is increasingly desperate to claim an honor student in the family." It was the kind of remark for which Molly was famous and it was part of the reason Nancy loved her. There was a kinship between them that was obvious, though inexplicable. Because of that kinship, Nancy worried, but not too much, about Molly's disregard for deadlines. Because of that kinship, Molly worried, perhaps too much, about Nancy's obsession with success, particularly when it resulted in stories about murder.

Molly wondered about ghosts. If there were ghosts at St. Anthony, she hadn't seen them. It seemed in her four years that there were very few places she had not been on the campus. She had even managed to peruse the "forbidden texts" in the roped off area, in the back of the top floor of the library. Wouldn't unhappy spirits hang around up there, if they were going to be anywhere?

After her father's death Molly often walked the campus in those in-between hours, as night yawned into morning. If Louise Porter was "crying out" then, why hadn't Molly heard it? Perhaps, Molly was too caught up with her own hauntings to notice any indigenous spirits. Louise Porter could have been desperately trying to get her attention and Molly was simply too self-absorbed to notice. Louise wouldn't have been the only one to complain about Molly's lack of attention, there were plenty of still-breathing critics of Molly on that topic.

Molly simply couldn't buy the ghost business, but then what had triggered Nancy's original interest in this case? "Nancy's more than likely right, but if there are ghosts, I doubt that even solving Louise Porter's murder could exorcise all of them from St. Anthony," Molly concluded. Placing a Judy Collins album on Nancy's stereo, she stretched out on the bed and waited for the chaste, clear notes to settle. Nancy seemed always to be right. If Molly would simply resign herself to that fact life might prove far easier.

"Hello, what are you doing here?" Nancy asked, as she swept into the room, throwing her books on the desk and lighting one of her ever-present Winstons. "How did you get in, anyway?" Nancy tended to fire several questions in rapid succession. In most cases, Molly was certain that it was more from habit than any genuine need to establish a dialogue.

"Thanks for the most gracious welcome!" Molly replied, allowing sarcasm to punctuate each syllable. "In answer to your first question, I'm attempting to visit the sick. I hear you get points for that and as you might suspect I'm in desperate need of points. Secondly, as far as my gaining entrance to your room, I accosted Polly Kuyper in the hall and she let me in with ye old Master Key. You know, it pays to be a friend of Polly with her 'keys to the kingdom.'

Nancy inserted paper into the typewriter and began typing furiously. Every movement staccatoed. That was Nancy's style and Molly marveled at it. Molly wrote everything on paper first, yellow legal pads or notebooks or scraps of paper she invariably misplaced.

"Do you want me to go?" Molly asked, sensing that Nancy was obviously too pre-occupied for company.

"No, stay," she commanded. "Am I supposed to be sick?" Nancy asked between puffs. It was strange that Nancy smoked. None of the other Kiernans seemed to do so and when Nancy was at home, she only smoked outside the house. If her parents knew she smoked, they never said anything, but then they never mentioned Kevin either. Molly thought they probably disapproved of both, but if they had ever voiced that disapproval or disappointment, even to Nancy, Molly was not aware of it.

"According to a certain revered gentleman of letters that we both know and love, nothing short of the Bubonic Plaque could keep you from his Journalism class." Molly liked to dabble in the dramatic. Nancy had that effect on her.

"Yes, well, I've got some cuts coming. It'll be all right," Nancy said defensively.

Certainly Nancy had cuts coming, but that wasn't the issue. Doc cared, that was all. Nancy of all people should understand that. Doc thought the world of her. "I was especially struck by Ms. Kiernan's insightful analysis of the story." Molly came to expect that every class would contain a Kiernan compliment and she was seldom disappointed. It wasn't that Doc gushed about the talent or intelligence of his students, it was the opposite really. There were Journalism seniors who had changed their majors after a few of Doc's critiques. It's just that Nancy was that good. Doc was impressed by her and that wasn't easy. Most of the Journalism students were good writers. They had come to St. Anthony for the most part, having been praised as great writers in their various high schools. (The big fish, small pond scenario.) The Journalism School at St. Anthony expected that you could write well as a freshman. It was designed to develop you into a better than decent at writer in everything by the time you graduated -- News, Sports, Features, Fiction, even Research. You had to be a "jack of all trades" and usually a master of one. Nancy seemed to be able to be a master of them all. Doc loved Nancy, but Molly always had a feeling that he liked Molly better. Molly, whose copy was late and frequently flawed – still caused him to smile. "Nice content" he would tell her. "Beautiful use of dialogue." Raising his eyebrows for effect, he would add, "Too bad I need the Rosetta Stone to read it."

"I'm sure it'll be fine. I think Doc was just genuinely concerned about you," Molly explained. "Why didn't you tell him about your story?" she asked.

Nancy whirled around. "He knows about the story. What did he say? What did *you* say?" She asked, with more than a hint of accusation in her voice.

"I don't think I said much of anything. I was just surprised. He seemed concerned that you weren't in class. He asked me if I knew why you were absent. I think I said I thought you might be too caught up in your investigative piece and he looked surprised, like he didn't have the faintest idea that you'd taken up grave robbing. We are talking about Doc-aren't we?"

Doctor Joseph Patrick Pascari, Chairman of the Department of Journalism at Saint Anthony University had been heir to his mother's Irish-blue eyes and his father's Continental charm. He seemed the perfect mixture of equal parts rogue and gentleman. His students loved him, his colleagues respected him and the community at large adored him.

Yet, it was unlikely that either their regard or his rather modest salary from St. Anthony kept him at the University. Pascari possessed an urbane charm blatantly out of place at so small and somewhat parochial an academic setting. *Something.* Molly couldn't put her finger on it, but something drove him, pushed him hard and then stopped him just short of the St. Anthony gates. He had been on the campus thirty years during which his contribution to the literary world had proved surprisingly small. It consisted of one short novel and a couple of textbooks. There should be something more than that--everything about Pascari suggested it. Molly had read the novel. It was interesting, but the Nobel committee definitely hadn't stayed up nights considering it. In addition, the book was twenty-three years old and the intervening years had aged both the book and the author dramatically. It was a good first novel--or seemed to be, but where was the rest of Doc? Where was the Great American Novel of which he seemed both capable and destined? Where were the anguish and passion that must have been present in order to make Doc the man he appeared to be?

"Do you think Doc ever had an affair?" Molly asked. She was in search of a rounder-outer of Doc's personality and like most people who have had no experience with them, Molly took great stock in romantic trysts. She believed that they provided the precise amount of guilt to inspire compassion and just enough regret to nurture wisdom.

Nancy stared at her friend in disbelief. "What would make you say that?" she asked in a tone both shocked and curious.

"I don't know. Granted it seems unlikely, daily communicant, Knight of St. John and all that business, but you can't tell anything from that. After all, Hitler was an altar boy or something like that, wasn't he?" Molly began thinking about Hitler. She knew he hadn't been Catholic, but she had heard about the altar boy rumor several times and always threw it out in conversation, just to see where it led. It was hard to imagine that Hitler had ever been a boy. Could young Adolf have collected frogs or played in a field or laughed and cried? Could he once have been frightened by monsters before he became one?

"Could we forget about Hitler and concentrate on Doc? Why would you suddenly, out of midair, ask me if I thought Doc had had an affair?" Nancy was growing evermore weary of Molly's constant tangent-travel. Sometimes it seemed that she was allergic to a straight answer.

"I was just thinking that he must have been really something. Okay, I know everything and everyone is something. I'll rephrase it. There's a little twinkle in his eyes, a wistfulness of manner, which makes me think he hasn't always been Saint Joseph," Molly concluded. Molly considered herself something of an artist, susceptible to wild theories and sensitive to the inner conflicts of those she met. Unfortunately, Molly thought everyone she met must be struggling with some great moral burden. Nancy wished that just occasionally Molly would be content with having acquaintances. She demanded more emotionally from people than she had a right to expect. Molly wanted to turn people inside out, like someone might turn a suit coat inside out to check the lining. Molly was always checking human linings. It could be presumptuous and tiresome!

Nancy laughed. "I love it. Typical Monaghan hard evidence. A certain twinkle in a man's eyes makes him an adulterer. Good Lord, he's fifty-six years old. Maybe he's got cataracts. I hope to God he never develops a limp. I'd be afraid to think what you would consider him to be then."

Molly admitted there wasn't much credence to her theory, but you could nevertheless tell a great deal about a person from his eyes, the "windows of the soul." Some nun had described eyes that way. Molly had forgotten the nun, but she remembered the quote. She was better with words than with faces. Words, phrases and mottoes--she clung to them, repeated them often in little, quiet places of her mind. She retreated to those places in hard times and let the words comfort her.

"Do you want to go to Mass?" Nancy asked. Nancy had recently embraced the faith. Hell, she had not merely embraced it. She had wrestled it to the ground and made it "cry uncle". For awhile, Nancy was "Praise Jesusing" the immediate world. Suddenly, a few months earlier Nancy had gotten caught up in an evangelist movement that was sweeping college campuses. If ever Bible thumping and the like were out of character, it was with Nancy. It was like Machiavelli meets Billy Graham. Nancy's initial fervor had quickly dissipated, but in the interim, she had become a daily communicant. Molly had always been one, at least at school. Over summer vacations, Molly was lucky to fulfill her Sunday obligation. She was grateful for Nancy's company at Mass, especially after Nan stopped chanting "Praise Jesus."

"What if Father Benedict says it?" Molly protested. The very name sent shivers down her spine. Father Benedict stuttered. That might have been all right, except apparently somewhere along the line he had learned to slow down in order to avoid stuttering. It didn't work. Father Benedict still stuttered, but now he sounded like a record being played at the wrong speed. He gave to each syllable its own special agonizing sound.

"So?" Nancy sneered. Sometimes Molly could be unreasonably difficult. Molly went to daily Mass, regardless of who celebrated it. She was one of the most deeply religious people Nancy had ever encountered and the least likely person to admit it. Molly was practically a closet Catholic. She constantly joked about her religion, treating the sacrosanct with irreverent humor. It made her feel vulnerable when people realized in what high esteem she held her church. Molly thought that Nancy should understand. Nancy did, but it occasionally annoyed her, nevertheless.

"*So*" Molly explained, "Father Benedict takes forever to get through a Mass and *so* we'll have to listen to a sermon that is as far removed from logic as it is from comprehensible English and *so* you might want to reconsider today's attendance at Mass."

."Molly, you're sacrilegious," Nancy concluded, without trying to hide her chagrin.

"It's hunger, not sacrilege! Last time we were unlucky enough to get "Beat-it-out Benny," we missed getting to the dining hall altogether. If Kevin hadn't delivered a pizza to us, we would have starved." Molly tended to employ hyperbole as everyday language.

The two friends walked toward the Friary Chapel in silence. That happened more than once to Nan and Molly--a brief respite from one another. It seemed fair. There would be an argument about politics or writing or even literature and the two friends would spend a few days apart. There would be no bad feelings or hostility, just a little distance. Both had different circles of friends. Nancy had her new "God Squad "friends, who Molly considered fanatics. Their over-zealous proselytizing made Molly more than a little uncomfortable. At Nancy's urging she had attended one of their meetings. When the student in charge couldn't find the list of readings for that night, he claimed that "evil spirits were planting obstacles in his way." If he were correct, then Molly had been plagued by those spirits for a lifetime and it had been simply unfair of her mother to accuse her of being heedless. Besides Brother Germaine who was in charge of the God Squaders sent shivers up Molly's spine. He spoke in tongues and presumably drove out demons.

Brother Germaine was tall and lean, his dark brown eyes stared out from a pock marked face that though not handsome in features, was unusually attractive. He possessed an aura of other worldness. The problem was that Molly wasn't sure what that world was. His fervor and eloquence had attracted many of the Saint Anthony students to the Charismatic Movement that he led on campus. Nancy interviewed Brother Germaine for a profile series she wrote for the school newspaper. What started as research and curiosity turned into personal zeal. Nancy was sure that Molly would join the Charismatic Movement. She convinced Molly to attend a Holy Hour. Brother Germaine seemed very bright and at times he shifted from ethereal to frenetic. His sermon was alive with raw emotion, no one could doubt his sincerity or faith, but his talk of demons made Molly finger the rosary in her coat pocket.

When Nancy pressed her to join the movement Molly explained that she preferred sinners to saints and left it at that. Nancy's God Squad friends thought Molly was at best a bad influence and at worst an instrument of the devil. They were not amused when they asked Molly if she had been reborn and she quipped, "No thanks. I'm still recovering from the first time." They prayed for Molly, but warned Nancy of her continued friendship. That may have been the impetus for Nancy's disenchantment and distance with the Charismatic movement.

Occasionally, one of Molly's friends might comment that she thought Nancy seemed a little stuck up. Nancy might accuse one of Molly's friends of being neurotic or inane, but neither Molly nor Nancy would be "warned" away from their own friendship.

Daily Mass in the Friary had become an essential element in Molly's day. She feared that it was the *location* of the Mass more than the actual celebration of the Liturgy itself that brought her back each day. Molly had been a junior in high school when she first visited the St. Anthony campus. Her Journalism Club visited annually and shadowed Journalism Majors. She had heard about the St. Anthony Journalism program. She knew she wanted to write and she admired the Franciscan philosophy, but it was that first visit to the Friary Chapel that captured her heart and inspired her to fill out the endless loan and financial aid forms required to attend the University.

She was awed by the blend of polished wood and marble, yet beyond that, she was struck by an aura of piety which enveloped this place. Here was a refuge for serious praying, for no-nonsense repentance, simple and startlingly beautiful. It was an easy, natural place to worship God. This was true even in the face of the insufferable Father Benedict. Molly took some comfort in that, as she heard the familiar voice intone "In the N-N-N-Name of the F-F-F-Father.

An hour and fifteen minutes later, Molly and Nan were sitting at a table in the all but abandoned dining hall. Molly forked a pile of grease-coagulated potatoes and wondered if gravy anywhere else could be classified as a solid. Her mood was not pleasant.

"So, what made you cut class today?" she asked.

"I was busy," Nancy mumbled. "Did you really think I was sick?"

"Well, it could happen. It is the middle of winter and you have been burning the candle at both ends. Doc seemed upset about it. He said to give his get-well wishes."

"Is that all he said?" That was all Nancy: Get to the point, the old "Any messages for me?" attitude.

"I don't know. Let's see, in class, we discussed the first amendment business about protecting your source and that sort of thing. You're familiar with the variety. Let's see, oh, yeah, he warned that all outstanding assignments are due on his desk by next week. I think that may have been primarily for my benefit. Per usual I'm a little late." The only time Molly's assignments weren't late were when they never saw daylight at all.

"Me, too," Nancy admitted. "I'm behind in everything."

"Everything?" This was incredible. Nancy not only met deadlines, she made it her trademark to beat them. When everyone else was busy developing outlines, Nancy was handing in perfectly typed copy. "

How come?" Molly asked, finally aware that something was terribly out of sync. Nancy paused. It was confidence time. She took on that confessional pall which indicates that what is about to be uttered is of enormous consequence.

"I'm scared, Moll. I'm so scared that I can't function." She stared down at the table as she spoke. There was a slight tremor in her voice. She appeared smaller than Molly had ever seen her, as if everything was tightened up, as if she had closed herself up as far as she could. Nancy Kiernan was not a shark now. At this moment she was just a terrified human being, terribly small and fragile. Whatever sense of warning that grabs people at movies and makes them yell, "Don't go in there." That particular foreboding of dark places that is instinctive and unmistakable, hit Molly full force. "No, don't," Molly shouted internally, "Stop, run back to the places of light. Run to the people who love you." Molly stared at her friend. She tried to see beyond the defenses. In a real crisis, Molly knew that could be done. She didn't buy Nancy's hard evidence arguments. Molly could see the genuine terror in her friend, she could feel it.

"It's this Louise Porter business, isn't it?" Molly said finally. Molly had always been a little uneasy about the project. She had tried to convince Nancy not to pursue it, but once Nancy decided to do something, it was never any good to argue.

"Molly," Nancy whispered, "I think I'm close to finding out who did it."

"Whoa. Back up. Media Res--Time and place. Molly immediately went to her rulebook, that section of her brain reserved for guidelines. She was sitting with a friend in the middle of a dining hall on a Catholic campus. She should be complaining about teachers, confessing her perpetual sexual frustration or discussing any other suitable conversational topic. Nancy instead was talking about murder. This day was quickly turning into a scene from a bad B-movie. "Murder at St. Anthony." Stop. Murder belonged to the late news, with folks who settled disputes with shotguns, unlucky drug dealers or people with unfortunate family connections. It did not belong here. Nancy had crossed over into dangerous territory. She had delved too deeply into an old and ugly, albeit interesting, piece of local history.

"You might have uncovered a murderer? This is crazy. You've got to give this up. Even if you think you know who did it, what's the point? Why not just forget about it?" Molly suggested.

"Brilliant, Monaghan! Just how am I supposed to do that?" complained Nancy with her best Joan of Arc tone. Nancy was all martyr now. She believed her own fantasies about being a great seeker of truth. It was bull-ditty. Worse than that, it had suddenly turned into extremely dangerous bull-ditty!

"It's easy and relatively painless," Molly explained. "You simply compile everything you have concerning the late, not so lamented, Louise Porter and meet me behind the dorm. Then we build a little fire and sing camp songs."

Nancy shook her head vehemently. "No."

"Yes." Molly insisted. "Then you write some harmless piece about waste in the campus food budget and enjoy the Christmas recess, like everyone else."

"I'd like to, Molly, but I can't. It's as if owed some kind of moral debt to Louise Porter. I can't explain it exactly, but I have to see it through." Molly wondered if she couldn't reach Nancy, perhaps someone else could--maybe Kevin or Father Tom or Doc. Maybe Molly should call Mr. Kiernan and have him insist Nancy forget this and come home. Nancy worshipped her father. Molly was sure he could get to her when no one else could. Nancy would be angry, but this was worth a little anger. It would be better to have Nancy angry than frightened or in danger. Nancy had gone off the deep end. Maybe she was having some kind of breakdown. First, the Praise Jesus crowd and now this. *"moral debt to Louise Porter…"*

"Really, Nan, a 'moral debt to Louise Porter?' What are you thinking? You don't owe anything to anybody. We're Seniors. We're six months from graduation and you can more or less write your own ticket after that. You've worked like a Trojan for four years - and you've got the transcript to show it. Just slide out of here. Are you even listening to me?"

Obviously Nancy wasn't. She was looking at Molly without focusing. That happened sometimes with Nancy. She seemed to look beyond the person with whom she was talking, as if her attention was somewhere else. It often was.

"Molly, would you do me a favor?" Nancy asked softly.

"Name it." There wasn't anything Molly wouldn't do for Nancy. Well, she might not kill someone or deal drugs but short of that, Nancy didn't need to ask. It was a given.

"Will you take a look at what I've got? It's possible I'm just too close to this thing. Maybe I'm chasing shadows. Maybe I've become too paranoid over the whole business. If after you've gone through the research you still think we should have the bonfire, I'll not only supply the material, I'll bring the marshmallows. Deal?"

A solution. A gift from God. Molly would take a cursory look at the Porter stuff and recommend forgetting the entire project. Nancy would be satisfied and everyone could go home and enjoy Christmas.

"It's a deal," Molly said. "But I can't do it right away. I have a Latin Etymology final tomorrow for which I know nothing, nada, nihil--anyway, you see my problem. It's my personal belief that Latin is what buried the Roman Empire--Nero and the Christians just had bad press."

"Please, Molly. It's important." The ache in Nancy's words seemed to dwarf the stature of a two thousand year old language. There really was never any question. Given the choice between doing a favor for a friend and fulfilling an individual responsibility, Molly would always choose to do the favor. It was a basic flaw in her character.

"Yes, okay. I'll stop over at your dorm later and pick up the material. As long as I'll be pulling an all-nighter anyway, I might as well have something interesting to read." Molly would, once again, let Nancy call the shots. Nevertheless, she thought some serious counseling might be in order. "You know," she cautioned, "if you really have uncovered something, you should have gone to the police with it. It's their job." There was, Molly reasoned, an order of things. The Church took care of souls, doctors and fitness freaks worried about health and the police were in charge of murder. They possessed both the time and the expertise. After all, it wasn't as if St. Anthony University and the nearby town of Sweet Valley was a hotbed of criminal activity. Occasionally, the local constabulary would grab a student holding a nickel-bag or harass a retired Mafia chieftain residing in reasonable obscurity just outside town. If there was anything to this Porter case it belonged to them. Nancy should be cognizant of that and act accordingly.

"You should let them handle it," Molly advised.

"I don't think they'd listen to me. It's not like I had concrete evidence. It's more conjecture and gossip. It's just a gut-feeling, really." Nancy admitted.

"So you figured you'd consult the resident expert on gut-feelings and gossip?" Molly attempted to appear offended. In truth, she was pleased in the confidence Nancy placed in her.

"Molly, if you're fishing for a compliment, you're not going to get one. You know I value your opinion, as both a writer and a friend. This time, though, there's more to it than that. This involves someone you know…"

"Somebody I know. Wait, I've got it. It's my Etymology Prof. It would be just like that old classics scholar to render some poor soul lifeless. He does it to me every class. I can see it now. 'Louise Porter, can you give me the etymological basis for homicide? No? Then I must provide you with a practical example.' What did the old boy do, brutally conjugate her to death?"

"Molly, this is serious." Nancy was definitely not open to levity on this topic.

"I was being serious! For a moment, I believed that through some miracle I would be saved from this god-forsaken exam tomorrow. Now you're going to ruin it all by telling me the butler did it."

"There's no butler and while you're at it, will you do one more favor for me?"

Molly groaned. "Speak, Master."

"Don't tell anyone about this. Do you understand? Not anyone!"

"Nancy, come to reality, will you? This is St. Anthony, not the Orient Express." Molly wondered if Nancy had pushed too hard, if perhaps her friend was dangling over a precipice that could leave you scuffling down the corridors in paper slippers.

"Humor me," Nancy said firmly.

"All right," Molly promised, although she was tired of doing precisely that.

"Promise?"

Molly thought perhaps Nancy would require a blood oath.

"Scout's honor," she said.

"Molly, you were never a scout, were you?" Nancy said accusingly.

Molly winked. "So, I lie," she confessed smilingly. I was a Sodalist – a devout member of Our Lady's Sodality.

"And did Our Lady's Sodality have a pledge?"

"Yes, but no cookies. I think we should have had cookies. Maybe, rosary bead-shaped cookies that we could sell by the decade instead of the dozen. Yep, no cookies, that was the downfall of Sodality. I'm sure of it.

On the way back to her dorm, Molly thought about her Sodality days. She still had the pin she wore on her high school uniform and the Miraculous Medal. They were home in some memory box. Maybe over Christmas she would look for those. The medal especially might come in handy.

CHAPTER II

Halfway through the eighth chapter of her Latin Etymology textbook, Molly leaned back from her desk and growled. Molly rather liked Church Latin, full of Kyries and Christes, ("If you want dominoes and biscuits call et cum spiri 2-2-0(tu tuo)") but not this stuff. This was simply a leftover from the crowd who, when they weren't running around in togas, amused themselves by feeding Christians to circus animals. She never managed to cultivate much enthusiasm for Ancient Rome. This disdain had always proved problematic.

Once, in high school, she had risked expulsion and possibly excommunication by suggesting that Cicero had an unnatural attraction to youthful members of his own gender. Her Latin teacher thought another year of Latin III might change Molly's opinions. "Oh times, Oh customs " Suddenly Molly was overcome with thirst. Something very cold and respectably alcoholic might exorcise old ghosts. Since she had promised to stop over at Nancy's anyway, she might as well convince Nan to adjourn to the skellar and, as Kevin would say, "imbibe liberally."

Outside, it was obvious that Christmas had come early to St. Anthony. Everywhere colored lights decorated windows and doorways. The landscape was layered in deep snow and along the footpaths couples passed, huddling together as much for shared warmth as mutual affection. Molly thought it would be hard to leave this place. She had grown too used to it--to the green beauty of it in the spring and summer, the remarkable colors in the fall and the stark, white winter of this campus. She shuddered.

She was getting too Christmas cardy. That's what Kevin would say. "Take warning! That kind of thinking will lead you to a string of bad school anthology poems and to inspiring verses for greeting cards that glitter." Molly must run from such dangerous thoughts like a mailman fleeing from a Doberman or for that matter like anyone fleeing a Doberman. Still, it was Christmas and regardless of Kevin O'Connor's cynical advice. There was nothing inherently wrong with sentimentality. It is, after all what separates us from the scientists.

On entering Nancy's dorm, the desk attendant handed Molly a note with Nancy's room key attached.

Dear Moll,

Kevin showed up on my doorstep with an invitation which I readily accepted. Who knows, perhaps a night of raw sex and/or incredible romance awaits. I could certainly use either! I promise to join you for Mass and dinner tomorrow and tell all. (If nothing good happens, I'll make something up.) Please leave the key at the desk when you're done. You know where everything is. Thanks. I owe you big time.

Love,

Nan

Splendid. While Nancy was snuggling up to Kevin, Molly would be sorting through material on a generation-old murder. Typical Monaghan luck. Of course, she could seek out Nancy and Kevin in the campus pub, but then what began as a date would turn into a gathering of friends and romance was fleeting enough. It wasn't sporting to help drive it away.

Nancy and Kevin, Kiernan and O'Connor--it sounded like a law firm. They were a strange couple, a rare combination. Most St. Anthony couples were more than openly affectionate. On any given night, the campus was a tangle of couples coupling. The only place that Molly hadn't witnessed fellow students in the throes of passion was the Friary Chapel. Although she had heard a rumor about either a very brave or very desperate couple who figured that the confessional was as good a place to commit sin as to repent of it. Molly didn't believe it. Even if you survived it physically, it would ruin you psychologically. It was still a good story though and Molly was addicted to good stories.

Molly found Nancy's files tucked safely away under some dirty laundry. Strange girl, this Nancy Kiernan. No one else hid files at St. Anthony. No one else kept files. No wonder Nancy had involved herself in a murder investigation. Why waste all this paranoia on typical campus trivia? Molly dumped the files into a plastic bag and scouted the room for anything else that might prove relevant. There were a few typed pages on Nancy's desk, but they were primarily melodrama. Besides, if things went badly and Nancy came home early, she might want to continue working on them. Molly knew she was missing something, but she just couldn't remember what it was. It was something about Nancy's method of writing. Something other than the files, but Molly couldn't put her finger on it. She didn't want to make a second trip before settling this matter, but her mind was not in high gear. She had this horrible suspicion that she would just get back to her own room, warm and relaxed and she would remember. While she concentrated, she threw Nancy's Judy Collins album on the top of the files. She might as well listen to something decent while pouring over this stuff.

It was no use. Nothing was coming through. Molly picked up the bag and was about to leave when she heard the knock at the door.

"Who's there?" she asked tentatively.

"Father Tom Madden."

Father Thomas Owen Madden -guaranteed both to inspire and absolve sin. Not a bad package. Thomas Madden, clear of eye, straight of jaw, quick of wit--where was that critical flaw that kept his birth from being celebrated every December 25th? It was to Father Tom that the boys came for sage counseling. It was to Father Tom that the girls revealed their secret longings. And it was to Father Tom that elderly alumni came to bequeath all of their worldly possessions to the University. He was everybody's darling and in this Molly was no exception. Yet Molly's attraction to Tom Madden differed somewhat from most other girls. She sensed something beyond the natural charm and innate beauty of the man, something very tender, lying close to the surface. In his eyes, sometimes in his voice, Molly perceived a loneliness, the evidence of a wound not quite healed. Naturally they had become friends. He provided the blessings and absolution. She provided laughter and a special brand of innocence. Both looked upon the other as very rare and very valuable.

Molly was sure that Tom would be the next President of St. Anthony. He had confided as much to her. She was glad she was graduating and wouldn't be here for that. She knew it was a promotion and a resume perk, but she was surprised that Tom would accept it. He was a great teacher. Molly had taken two of his theology courses. She loved the way that he humanized the faith. University presidents didn't teach. They weren't really a part of students' life. It was a waste to take Tom away from that. Nobody who saw him in a classroom or interacting with the students would have sentenced him to a future behind a desk or attending countless fund raisers.

Over the years Molly had many long walks with Tom. She was never surprised to see him in a St. Anthony sweatshirt and jeans in the middle of a touch football game or emerging a little the worse for wear from a Rugby scrum. He was always busy, but never too busy. "Walk with me," he'd say "I'm due at the Friary for Confession or I have to see if I can get the gym for a pick-up basketball game…". Molly had seldom seen him walking alone during the day. He always seemed to be with a student, laughing or talking seriously. . He was present to the students of St. Anthony University and as president he would not be. "Why not refuse?" Molly had asked.

Tom tugged on his Franciscan robe. "This. When I chose this outfit, I promised to do what I was asked. Obedience. Remember that rule?" Father Tom was all about rules: the rules of the Church and the Rules of St. Francis and even some self-imposed rules regarding dress and language and behavior.

He had long ago explained his iron-clad policy about never visiting a girl's dorm room. "People talk," he assured her, "and what they don't know, they make up." Perhaps he was a little paranoid, but then again, Catholics love to gossip about their clergy. Maybe it was a partial legacy of the Inquisition. Nothing is quite as sensational as a Church scandal. Thus, Father Tom's view on visiting a girl's dorm room appeared cautious but reasonable. With that in mind, Molly opened the door, wondering what would inspire this remarkable policy change.

"Molly, what are you doing here?" he asked, obviously surprised and perhaps more than a little annoyed.

"Great minds think alike. I was about to ask you the same thing"

How strange and uncomfortable he looked in the hallway. Molly was used to seeing Tom Madden, watching him on the altar or lecturing or granting absolution. She realized suddenly, that the same people look different in different situations. She decided to file that thought. Someday it might make its way into a novel or if the fates failed her it might fit on a tea bag tag.

"Is Nancy here?" he asked, unconscious of Molly's reverie. Okay, she thought, the old "I must be about my Father's business."

"No, she isn't. Do you want to come in for a minute or are you not allowed?" Molly asked tersely.

"What do you mean by that?" he mumbled as he walked into the room and proceeded to scrutinize the surroundings.

"It seems to me that you said that you had some rule about girls' rooms." Why was Tom here? Nancy's room, of all the rooms he might visit.. "Of all the gin joints …How did that go? That classic *Casablanca* line, *"Of all the gin joints in all the* what?

"Sometimes exceptions are warranted." Tom explained. His eyes searched the room as though he expected Nancy to be hiding in the corner.

"Father," Molly asked, "is there something I can do for you?"

"Maybe. What did you say you were doing here?"

I didn't, Molly thought. He didn't really have a right to ask. It was an odd question. Students were always in friends' rooms. Molly seldom locked her room. She would commonly come back from class or the library or the skellar to find a note on her desk and something borrowed or returned. Nancy chided her about her open door policy, but Molly was certain that her prize possessions, various Irish poetry and history books were unlikely to tempt anyone to break the seventh commandment. "What do you think the street value of *"The Poems of Thomas McDonough* might be?" she'd ask and Nancy would just shake her head. Father Tom was staring at Molly. She pointed to the bag. The album cover was clearly visible. "I'm stealing my neighbor's goods," she confessed.

"Judy Collins. Hmm. Did you break and enter to do it?" He asked.

"No, I'm not that accomplished yet. I have Nancy's key."

"You and Nancy are best friends, aren't you?" he asked.

"We're close." Molly objected to the exclusivity of bests.

"Then you should convince her to stop this," he said sternly.

Does that translate as, "Be out of town by sundown or else?" What gives? Molly thought. Nancy should stop *this* – what was this? Was it the story or something else? It had to be the story, but how was Father Tom connected?

"Pardon me, Father. What is Nancy supposed to stop?" Molly asked, more than a little confused.

"I'm serious Molly. You must know what she's been up to." Molly did know, but she had no idea what it had to do with Father Tom. Whatever that connection, Molly would rather not discuss it. She had never before lied to Father Tom. He had been her confessor and her friend, but Molly had promised Nancy to remain quiet about all of this and that commitment had to be honored. There were precedents. She gave Tom her most perplexed look. That was easy. Nothing since she answered the door had made any sense. She was Alice in the rabbit hole.

"I don't know that Nancy's been up to anything. Is there a full moon or something? Look, I'd love to stay here with you and continue this inane conversation, but I have a final tomorrow and I have to get back to my room and study." It's true, she thought. I have to get back to my half-eaten Danish and pot of coffee, back to cramming for a final, back to the familiar indigestion and lack of will power which has become an integral part of my existence. Molly was worried. Studying had never before appealed to her.

"I'll walk you back, if you like," Tom offered.

A Sleeping Dog

Molly shrugged. She didn't care if he walked her back to her dorm or not. Jerk. He shows up where he's not supposed to be and acts like it's an everyday occurrence. Then he starts making noises like a small town hood. For Christ's sake, the man was destined to be the next president of a decent-sized university. Why was he behaving so strangely? Obviously, Nancy had ruffled his feathers a little, but normally Father Tom Madden would welcome a challenge. Maybe the cynics were right. Maybe the priesthood created crazies. Too long alone, no wife, no kids, no over-due bills, no leaky trash bags. Maybe they went a little bonkers and as a result they caused their friends to do the same. They weren't only good candidates for nervous breakdowns--they were also carriers. It was beyond understanding. Molly needed a stiff drink and some salacious reading material, the mainstays of student life at St. Anthony.

The walk back across campus was quiet. Father Tom was obviously preoccupied. When they reached her dorm, Molly managed a polite goodnight and half-ran up the stairs to her room. She couldn't explain what was happening. Suddenly her pulse raced and it felt like the entire East German shot put team was seated on her chest. She tried to breathe, but each breath shot pain through her body. Maybe she was having a heart attack. Perhaps she was stroking out, but that didn't make sense. Wasn't twenty years old too young for something of major proportions? Wasn't there some unwritten law, which allowed for at least another ten years of serious bodily abuse? Still, she couldn't seem to focus. She managed to remove her coat and lie down on her bed. There in the darkness, the perspiration streaming down her back, Molly began making promises. "If I survive, if this is just some freak incident brought on by bad diet and whatever else combines to do this to people, I promise I'll be better. I'll cut down on everything: Less coffee, more salad. I'll even consider exercise and switch from white bread to that stuff that tastes like the soles of shoes." Everything raced together --pieces of memories, her family, Kevin, Nancy, Father Tom. They were swallowed by an urgency, a panic of emotion. Molly couldn't feel her arms or legs. She could only experience the pain in the center of her body. Each shallow breath strangled trying to escape. Relax, she thought. Calm. Each intake of breath felt like she was being punched in the chest. Could this be it? It must be indigestion. Finally the pain subsided. Molly hugged the pillow to her chest and took deep breaths. She thanked God. It's over and I'm okay. Maybe I have to be careful. It must be the caffeine and all the sugar. It couldn't be anything else. Molly decided to sleep for a while. She turned off the lights and fell into bed. "I'll just nap for an hour or so," she mumbled. As she closed her eyes, she noticed the plastic bag with Nancy's research. She had dropped it next to the bed.

CHAPTER III

Again. It had become necessary again. Taking the Bible, opening it to the page that had become so familiar, once again the killer began to read from Isaiah loud:

From the womb the wicked are perverted, astray from birth the liars gone. There is poison like a serpent's, like that of a stubborn snake that stops its ears, that it may not hear the voices of enchanters casting cunning spells. O God, smash their teeth in their mouths, the jaw teeth of the lion break, 0 Lord. Let them vanish like water flowing off; when they draw the bow, let their arrow be headless shafts. Let them dissolve like a melting snail, like an untimely birth that never sees the sun. Unexpectedly like a thornbush or like thistles, let the whirlwind carry them away. The just man shall be glad when he sees vengeance. He shall bathe his feet in the blood of the wicked. And men shall say, "Truly there is a reward for the just; truly there is a God who is judge on earth.

"Unexpectedly." Yes, she had not expected it. She had opened the door that morning, smiling, confident, scheming. She had not expected the knife. She had writhed on the floor, uttering small sounds, not even cries. Her wounded serpent's body. So lovely, so tempting in life, so still in death. The knife had opened up her ugliness. It had come again and again until there was more than enough blood to wash one's feet. Death in a whirlwind. Death from the hand of someone she had manipulated, someone she had used. Death to the temptress, the serpent. Then the rain had come. The rain of baptism, the rain of renewal. The knife had been kept. The weapon of justice. It had been wrapped in a table napkin, a reminder of that day and of the cost of sin. So many years ago. At first, there had been nightmares. Long nights thick with doubt and remorse, but that had passed. The scandal had died with the woman. So few knew the truth. The horror of lust and betrayal centered around one person. The woman died and the storm passed and the scandal had been buried with her. Her victims had survived, even prospered. The nightmares had faded, the doubt succumbed. St. Anthony had grown in size and prestige. There had been no public display of dirty laundry. The survivors had learned their lesson. They had steered clear of temptation. They had taught and counseled and inspired an entire generation of students. What was one life, as opposed to so many?

But once again, ruthless ambition would need to be extinguished. Once again, it would be necessary to protect this holy place and its people from the proud and arrogant spirit, which threatened the life around it. It would be necessary to crush the ugly head of the serpent once more. The beast must be exorcised. So much is required by the Lord. Abraham had prepared his own son for sacrifice. To be a soldier, to protect what one believes in, one must be willing to kill as much as to die. That is the harsh reality. "To whom much is given, much is required". It was simple, really. Afterwards, when the memory of it came, there was a sense of excitement, a rush. It was time to do it again. Time to be the executioner. The girl must be stopped. There was no other way. The blue St. Anthony jacket was taken from the back of the closet. Its hood pulled tight over the killer's head. The gloves were put on and the knife secreted beneath the jacket. There was nothing left now but to wait. Wait for that moment when the girl would be alone. When respecting nothing, fearing no one, she would venture into the darkness without protection. Then, the whirlwind would reap yet another. Perhaps that would end it. There would be no others so foolish, so haughty, not to realize that it is best to let the dead lie in peace. It is wisdom to let a sleeping dog lie.

Nancy and Kevin walked down the dark, narrow stairs to the St. Anthony Skellar. Kevin had remarked once that it should have been called the Cave instead of the Rathskellar. The stair case was so narrow that it was hard for students to exit while others were entering. Molly worried about a fire, but Kevin had discovered other doors and exits from the bar, that were wider and could easily accommodate a hurried leaving of the place if necessary. He, of course, had to show them to Molly one afternoon.

"More people should know about these." Molly commented.

"Why?" Kevin asked.

"Because of a fire or some other emergency."

"What other emergency, a nuclear holocaust or something? In that case, you don't need another exit. What's the age old advice: 'Bend over as far as you can and kiss your ass goodbye'?"

That must have made sense to her because Molly became a regular at the skellar, mostly accompanied by either Nancy and/or Kevin, but other times with other friends. Sometimes though, she would go alone, just after the skellar opened for the night and sit at one of the back tables and write. She would find a quiet, hollow space. Surrounded by a sea of voices and activity, she would discover a solitary island. Like her early morning walks or her occasional late night visits to the chapel, Molly found this time comforting and inspirational. She would take mental pictures to add to her memory of places and scenes to be used at a later time and she would reflect on the real stories that played out in these places.

Usually, by the time Kevin and Nancy arrived at the skellar, it was crowded with students, often most of the senior class, hunched over pitchers of beer, near-screaming to be heard over the blaring jukebox or bumping into one another on the miniscule dance floor. Tonight though, it was somewhat subdued. Kevin ordered a tuna sub, a pitcher of beer and two glasses of red wine. He asked Nancy if she wanted anything to eat, but she declined. They went to their usual spot in the back room, even though they could have easily conversed in the open area near the bar. Molly called their usual table, the office. One night, in September, much to Molly's chagrin, Kevin had carved their initials in the underside of the table top.

"It's really dead down here, tonight." Kevin remarked.

"Finals started this week. Don't you have any?" Kevin never seemed to worry about classes. Nancy had taken several courses with him and he barely seemed awake during class, he took minimal, if any, notes, yet had maintained a 3.5 GPA for four years. There were probably only a handful of people who knew how bright Kevin was or how funny. Nancy thought of the John Donne statement that, "No Man is an Island…" Donne didn't know Kevin. Who really knew Kevin? she wondered.

"I have a final Thursday in Russian History and I have a paper due in Sociology, but that's no big whup." He shrugged. "I'm beat from work though. The store's open 'til nine every night and tons of people want pictures restored and that kind of thing for Christmas. "

"Can you do that? …restore pictures" she added, when Kevin looked confused by the question.

"Jack's been showing me how, but mostly I watch the counter and take orders while he does all the big jobs. It's neat, though." Kevin admitted.

"Would you ever want to do that, for a career? Own your own shop?" Every Journalism major seemed to dream of a career as a war correspondent or a photojournalist or a network anchorman. Sometimes, though, they cast their future nets a little wider and wondered if they might not end up as teachers or sales people, writing copy for advertising or perhaps going on to study law. Journalism was one of those majors, like political science that worked as a frequent lead-in to a law career.

"I want to get a job on a paper, but there's no local paper at home. I may have to take a job doing something else." Kevin had been offered an opportunity to stay on at the camera shop and go for a Masters Degree, but he was ready to leave. Most of the Business Majors and Education Majors were going for Master Degrees, but neither Journalism, nor Photography was offered in Graduate School at St. Anthony. Besides Kevin needed to begin life in the "real world." That's how his father referred to it. His father had wanted Kevin to study medicine or business. He had not been happy with Kevin's choice of colleges or majors. Kevin had managed to attain a partial scholarship and paid his own tuition through student grants and loans. His father's attitude was: "your decision, your cost." Kevin was proud of his independence. It seemed, though, that things had never been great with his dad, at least not since puberty. It hadn't bothered much, especially in the last couple of years. Home was someplace he visited. St. Anthony was where he lived.

Now though, the dread of returning home without even a promise or much of a prospect of gainful employment loomed large in Kevin's thoughts. When he was with friends he could escape it for awhile.

He didn't talk much about his family. Nancy had met his parents one Parents Weekend at school. His mother was friendly and fussed over both her husband and her son. His father seemed quiet, thoughtful and almost preoccupied. He was a dentist. Nancy could easily imagine him in a white lab coat and mask. What most struck Nancy was that Kevin seemed nothing like his parents. She had discussed it with Molly. "Maybe he's adopted." Molly suggested.

"He looks just like his father." Nancy countered.

"That happens all the time" Molly said with authority. "One of my closest friends in grammar school was adopted and she was the image of her mother, her *adopted* mother. You could ask him." Nancy did.

"Hell, no." Kevin shook his head. "My mother nearly died in labor. I was ass backward or something. What made you think that?"

"You're different than your parents."

"My mother says I'm a lot like my father. She claims that's why we argue all the time. She's probably right." Kevin surmised.

"It could just be that father and son thing – very Dostoyevsky."

"Right. My life is definitely something out a Russian Novel or maybe the Guinness Book of Records or Our Town." They had laughed then. They started naming stories and matching them to friends.

Nancy thought of that conversation. Kevin was likely not excited about going home, especially since it might mean working at something else other than writing or photography.

"You could come to Albany. I'm sure my father could hook you up with something." Nancy had thought of it several times. She knew that her family connections could be used to help both Molly and Kevin get started in pretty much any career they chose. Molly would never leave home, though. Well, at least not now, although Nancy wouldn't be surprised if later when her brothers were older Molly took to the road. There were lots of opportunities where Molly lived and the Monaghans were not exactly unknown in that community. Molly's hometown reminded Nancy a little of Tammany Hall. She figured Molly would do okay, but Kevin came from what used to be described as "a one horse town." Most of its citizens had worked in a sawmill that had just about closed down over the last decade. Nancy didn't like to think of Kevin working at the mill or seeking work where there was none. She was sure he would benefit from a larger venue for his enterprises, Nancy just wasn't sure how he would respond to an offer of help. Kevin was fiercely independent. For the first time Nancy worried about their romantic relationship. She hoped that it wouldn't complicate Kevin's "after school" possibilities. If they were just friends, she was sure that he wouldn't resist her offer to help. Well, she was fairly confident that he wouldn't have.

"Have you decided, yet, what you're going to do?" Kevin asked. They had talked at length about the future. Nancy had been thinking about politics and also had applied to several law schools. All of the seniors had spent hours over the last few months, applying for grad schools and law schools and internships. They had been busy writing resumes, seeking guidance and practicing interview techniques.

"I received my acceptance for SUNY at Albany Law School. I think I might do that." Nancy said.

"That sounds promising. What kind of law, do you know?" Kevin could see Nancy as a lawyer. No question. He didn't think she was much into it though. She liked writing and she was good at it. but then there was a lot of writing in the law, he thought. She could also write some book on the Constitution or something. There was International Law, too. He wondered if somebody could earn a living practicing that. Maybe she'd end up as a judge. It was easy to envision Nancy as "Your Honor".

Nancy appeared thoughtful, brows appropriately furrowed, "I don't know. I'm not sure, I'll even stay in Albany. There's a little time before we have to decide. I was thinking I'd visit the campus over vacation before I make a decision." It was unlike Nancy not to have a plan. "I might take a shot at a Congressional internship. That would mean, at least the summer in Washington, maybe a year. I might apply to Georgetown Law."

"So, if I went to Albany, you wouldn't be there?" Kevin had thought about going to Albany or New York City. He had friends going to both cities. He would have to make a decision soon, but each time he thought about the future, it seemed more surreal. If Nancy were in Albany, then Kevin would go there. It wasn't because he had any illusions about ending up with Nancy, but they could still be friends. That might not turn out as good as it looked. Nancy was different at home. He had visited there last summer when Molly was staying. The Kiernans were courteous, but not that friendly. Of course, he didn't know if they knew that he and Nancy were involved. Nancy had introduced him simply as Kevin, not as my boyfriend. He realized that they never used those terms, boyfriend and girlfriend. Still, regardless of the terminology, Kevin was pretty sure that the Kiernans knew what was going on and they were not exactly thrilled by it. Who could blame them? Kevin had sisters and he didn't want to think about meeting their boyfriends. Regardless of how polite Kevin had been, "Hi, I'm Kevin and I'm diddling your daughter." is probably what Mr. Kiernan had heard when he was introduced.

Besides everyone was probably different at home than they were at school. No one had ever visited his home. He imagined he was different among his sisters. At home, he was the big brother and the only son. He was alternately adored and envied by his sisters. He wouldn't have admitted it, but he missed them. Regardless of his post-graduation plans Kevin would spend the summer at home. Kevin was used to being surrounded by women. The first couple of years at St. Anthony, he hated living in the guys' dorm. At first, it was fun, but after a bit, though his male pride would never allow him to confess this, he longed for a cleaner, quieter, more aromatic environment. He wondered if that's why his best friends from college were girls. He had lots of male buddies, but no one who was as close to him as Molly and Nancy.

"Albany would be okay. Do you think I could get a job at the Chronicle?" That would be great, he thought. He would be willing to owe the Kiernans big time if they could land him a job on the paper.

"I don't know, but you could maybe have a job someplace else and still work free-lance. You're good, Kevin. If a photojournalist position is what you want, I bet it won't take you long to get it." Nancy believed in Kevin. She and Molly often commented on the quality of Kevin's photography. They didn't compliment him often because he was uncomfortable with compliments and it invariably inspired some self-deprecating remark.

"I could talk to my dad about it over break" Nancy offered. "Think about it," she suggested.

He would think about it. The truth was that he had thought about it, but then like most things, he tabled it in favor of more immediate concerns.

"I thought we'd see Molly down here tonight. I haven't talked to her in weeks. What's going on with her? He missed Molly. He knew that everyone was busy, but usually Molly found time for friends. He was worried about her. She had been struggling this semester. She was taking three heavy writing courses and she was buried under work. Molly bled when she wrote. She stayed up all night, wringing out her soul for a page of copy.

During finals week the dining hall was open all night serving coffee and doughnuts to insomniac students. Kevin remembered stopping there, after the skellar closed one finals night last year. He not only could use some black coffee before he hit the road, but it was an opportunity to stock up on free doughnuts. He was surprised to see Molly sitting alone at a table. She looked terrible. She had been writing. He didn't know anyone else who wrote as well or for whom it cost as much.

"She's got a Latin Etymology final tomorrow. I think she was planning on cramming tonight." Nancy explained.

Kevin looked surprised. "She'll pass that, no problem. She took a sequence in Latin in high school, didn't she?"

"Yes. I also asked her to do me a favor." Nancy admitted. "I asked her to look over a piece I'm writing."

"That doesn't seem fair. You get to go out and she has to stay in and work—that's a sweet deal." Kevin said kiddingly.

"Hey, it isn't like I take advantage of Molly. I do plenty for Molly, you know." The truth was Nancy felt guilty about including Molly in all of this. It had been Nancy's choice to investigate Louise Porter's murder. Molly hadn't liked the idea from the very beginning and now Nancy was throwing Molly right in the middle of it. It was just that she could trust Molly. She knew she would tell her the truth. If Molly thought Nancy was really unto something, she would tell her to keep writing regardless of the cost and if Molly said to forget it, Nancy would. That was the deal. Nancy should never have started this. There were a thousand ways she could have written the piece without really investigating the crime itself. It was just when she got into it – it seemed like nobody else cared about the murder. She couldn't just write off the taking of a human life because the investigation might embarrass the University. Wasn't that the real purpose of writing? Molly always said: "It's our job to ask the big questions, to seek and write the truth as we see it." It was naïve perhaps, maybe pompous and unrealistic but Nancy believed it. She had unwittingly ripped open an old, ugly, infected scar and no matter how it hurt the University, it needed to be aired out. Louise Porter didn't deserve to be forgotten, her life unspoken, her death ignored. No human being deserved that.

Kevin laughed, "Relax, I was just teasing. How come you're so sensitive all of a sudden?"

"I'm sorry, Kevin. I'm just not myself. Anyway, I was invited for an evening with this guy I really like and I couldn't pass that up." Nancy smiled. She meant it. She needed Kevin at that moment. She needed his voice and his humor and hands covering hers. She loved his hands and back of his neck and his shoulders…She loved his presence. It wasn't just sex, it was the touch, the spontaneous embrace, the genuine affection, the confidence he gave her, his earnest belief in her value and ability. Lots of couples were constantly entwined. That was not Kevin's style. There were few "PDAs" as Kevin referred to "public displays of affection" but when they were alone Kevin was uncharacteristically open and surprisingly tender. There was also a conversational intimacy that always made Nancy feel comfortable and totally free to be whoever she was at that moment. She wondered if she should tell Kevin about the Louise Porter mess. Maybe the three of them, Kevin, Molly and she should go through the research together and discuss what to do. Right now. They could go to Molly's room and the three of them could thrash it out and then maybe they could have that bonfire Molly suggested earlier. This would be a perfect night for a bonfire – so cold and crisp. Then they could help Molly cram for Etymology. For a moment, it all seemed doable. No. Kevin had enough on his plate. She would have dinner tomorrow with Molly and they would do what needed to be done.

"Well, whoever you are, I hope this guy isn't just trying to get you drunk and have his way with you. " Kevin warned.

"Do you think he might only want me for my body?"

"It's a nice body. I wouldn't be surprised," he said knowingly. Nancy did have a nice body, not the kind that would cause wolf whistles or incite lascivious remarks, but that was mostly because it wasn't what captured your attention. Kevin was stunned the first time they were together. He was not a virgin, not technically, but Kevin had never been invested emotionally in his bed partners or back seat or back room partners as the case might be. He sometimes liked the girl and sex was the culmination of several dates, more often, though it was the getting together at the end of a party or a night's drinking. He had never taken the time to really look at a girl's body. With Nancy, he had done that. While she slept and the first light of morning came through the bedroom window and draped her face, he studied her and he was amazed. He sometimes would lift the sheet and commit to memory each line and curve of her naked body in repose. He wanted to photograph her like that, but he knew that would break all the rules. Kevin was no fool. She was so beautiful, but no camera would capture the feel of her skin, the energy and excitement, the strength and youth, her generosity in sharing this with him. He couldn't find the words to express what he felt. Once, he had whispered, "You're beautiful." Nancy had looked shocked and then one tear, just one had escaped the corner of her eye. Sometimes in the middle of a heated argument with Nancy about religion or politics, the memory of that tear would creep up on him and Kevin would forget his point. He would just shrug and move onto another topic.

Kevin and Nancy stayed at the Skellar almost until closing. Nancy had a third glass of wine and Kevin managed to share his beer with a friend who stopped by the table to say hello and ended leaving an hour later. Nancy walked with Kevin to his car. It would take a while for the car to warm up, so they decided to do the same. Kevin tried to persuade Nancy to go to his apartment. He could get her back to the dorm tomorrow in plenty of time for class. It had been weeks since they had been together. Nancy realized that it had been some time, but she was fairly certain that Kevin had not been sexually abstinent. Nevertheless, it was tempting.

For one thing, Kevin's apartment was removed from campus and she needed time away -- away from this whole mess surrounding the late, not properly lamented, Louise Porter, away from the incredible hypocrisy and suspicion she seemed to be uncovering everywhere. In addition, there was the ever-present attraction of sex. A little time and energy spent in that direction might just put the rest of her life in proper perspective. It might take the edge off.

She was not in love with Kevin. There had never been that spark of excitement she had always believed accompanied romance. Perhaps she would never love anyone. Maybe it was impossible to let down her defenses. Maybe. Someday. But not now. No, this wasn't love. It was sex., but sex wrapped in a blanket of comfort, of camaraderie and of friendship. She was aware, too, that Kevin did not love her. At least, not in the "Let's get married and have a couple of kids and a two-career home" kind of love. It was more like "Let's get together and enjoy each other occasionally." There was no lifelong commitment. Their relationship was neither pure lust nor undying love. It was just a mutual fondness and that suited them equally. The prospect of waking up in Kevin's arms was certainly attractive, but the thought of a restful night in her own bed won out. There was really too much work to finish before semester break. "Kevin, let's postpone this until the weekend" she suggested finally.

"If you're sure," Kevin mumbled. Kevin definitely wanted to be with Nancy tonight, but he couldn't appear too anxious. Even if he was of the opinion that if he didn't experience some mutual affection soon, he might suffer irreparable damage to both body and libido. One had to be careful. Several of his friends were becoming engaged. It had reached epidemic proportions and they had not yet reached the very dangerous night of New Year's Eve or the amorous month of February. Everywhere guys were frantically putting down-payments on rings and traveling outrageous distances on weekends to meet prospective in-laws. There was no doubt that these were perilous times for St. Anthony seniors. Graduation and post-graduation could be scary.—job hunting, moving to new places, trying new things. Sometimes the prospect of sharing all that with someone you were close to, someone you could count on, became too damn inviting. Kevin didn't know quite what road lay before him but he was certain he didn't want to start off on the road by walking down an aisle.

Nancy seemed to be like-minded when it came to marriage, but you still had to be careful. You couldn't get too sentimental or involved. The senior class was stock full of girls who had expressed the very identical viewpoint as Nancy, but suddenly, those same girls were picking out china patterns. Better to leave well enough alone. If Nancy didn't want to be with him, it was her choice. Be a nice guy and forget about it. What was it Molly always said? "Life is too short to waste time worrying." They kissed good-bye and Nancy watched as Kevin's relic of a car sputtered away toward town.

Such a clean night. It felt like Christmas. In a week she'd be home. Maybe she'd get some skiing in over vacation. She loved the feel of downhill skiing – the rush, the speed of it. Nancy couldn't remember a time when she didn't ski. Her father had taught her. When she was very little, he would make her practice on piles of snow that had been removed from behind their house. Later, she would go with him and her brothers for week-end ski trips. Her mother almost always stayed at home to chair some social event. Once, Nancy broke her ankle in a bad fall. She remembered the look of terror on her father's face. Her father always appeared so confident, so in charge. All the color drained from his face. They were supposed to go to Aspen the following week, but her father cancelled the trip. He stayed at home at her beck and call. Her mother too, was uncharacteristically affectionate and solicitous during Nancy's recuperation.

Skiing or not, she was going to enjoy this Christmas. She was going to share time with her family. She had nieces and nephews that she seldom saw. Nancy remembered to send them birthday presents and an occasional greeting card. She liked to send them a card for no reason, in particular or a children's book or unique little toy. "I loved to get mail when I was little," she explained. The last four years had been so busy, it sounded trite but it was as if the years had flown past. In other ways, her time at St. Anthony had been a separate lifetime. This place had taken her over. Nancy had capitulated without regret. She had found something here, a sense of belonging and achievement. Almost from the beginning, from her acceptance interview, she had loved it. St. Anthony University --.It was so beautiful. Even now in the dead of winter, when so many places looked stark and hostile, this campus possessed a certain charm--you could see it, you could hear it on the crunch of the snow beneath your feet. Then Nancy heard something else. It was almost imperceptible, but it was her name. It was whispered, but it carried the way even a whisper seems like a shout on a cold night. Nancy turned toward the voice and saw the knife come at her. A scream caught in her throat as the blade ripped open her neck and chest. She tried to fight, but she was paralyzed. It came to her then, something from another lifetime. Something left-over from a kid in a Buster-Brown haircut and an over-sized school uniform. The stammerings of a prayer: "0 my God, I am heartily sorry." The knife stabbed again and again, Nancy's mind stuck to the prayer. In a few seconds it was over. Nancy Eleanore

Kiernan was heartily sorry and Nancy Eleanore Kiernan was dead. The killer took Nancy's scarf and carefully wrapped it around the knife. Then the person who had called Nancy's name so softly and ended her life so viciously, walked noiselessly away into the still, cold night.

CHAPTER IV

Someone was shouting her name. In her haste to open the door, Molly tripped over her shoes and smashed into the closet. "Nice move," she mumbled, as she reached for the lights. It was still dark when she finally opened the door. Marion Schmidt was waiting. "Is the sky falling?" Molly asked nonchalantly. She was used to Marion's hysterics. It was her trademark. Marion worked for the campus radio station and had a library of practice tapes with "Marion Schmidt live on-the-scene reporting. " everything from Papal elections to Presidential Assassinations. "One can never be too prepared." Marion was a life understudy, waiting breathlessly backstage for her moment of glory.

"Have you heard?" Marion asked as she scurried into the room. "It's incredible, isn't it? Of course it's not really incredible. I always thought something like this would happen. The men around here, if you could call the males at St. Anthony men, are all perverts! The priests feed you all that garbage about our boys, like this was Boy's Town. Good Catholic youth. Residents-on-duty all night long. A lot of good residents did her. Do you think she was raped? I bet she fought him off and that's why he went that far. Some Public Relations for St. Anthony. I wonder who's going to cover it for the station? I'm really the one they should get, but I bet they'll have one of those upstarts from the Sophomore class do it. It isn't fair they get all the good stories." Molly couldn't take it any longer. "Marion, what the hell are you babbling about?"

Molly hated being abruptly awakened. She liked to lie in bed and let her body slowly adjust to the realization that it must move. She liked to stretch and yawn and turn into wakefulness. She hated being blathered at, particularly by Marion and particularly at whatever god-forsaken hour this was.

"What time is it?" Molly demanded. Time and place were important. They gave a central focus, a base from which to work.

"It's five-thirty. Are you listening? You never listen to me. You're like everyone else. You're not even awake, are you? You were going to pull an all-nighter so you could pass Latin. What happened to your good intentions? You were asleep just now, weren't you? That's why it took you so long to answer the door. Molly, I can't believe you've reached the level where you sleep in your clothes. That's disgusting!"

"Life can be very disillusioning, Marion," Molly stated flatly.

"Well, I bet you're sorry. You slept through the biggest story to hit St. Anthony in this revered institution's long and proud history," Marion gloated. "But maybe you were lucky. You were out earlier this evening, I know, because I came up here to provide moral support for your long hours of study and you were gone. Suppose you had run into this maniac? I mean, it could have been you. It could have been anyone! Who knows who the next victim will be? Believe me, I know this type of societal parasite, they don't stop at one.' Molly suspected that Marion's knowledge of such "types" was limited to a few strangler biographies and an intro class in Psych.

"Who is it?" Molly asked quietly.

"The perpetrator?" Marion had definitely watched too many television police shows.

"The victim, Marion, for Christ's sake, who got hurt?"

"Not hurt," Marion said snidely, "Killed. Some girl was stabbed to death tonight."

Clare Tracey arrived. My God, Molly thought, everybody's up and running. Clare treated Marion to her best "Why not return to your home planet" look. "Smitty, somebody was looking for you." Marion hated to be called Smitty. Knowing that, Clare refused to call her anything else.

"Was it someone from the radio station?" Marion asked frantically. "Maybe they want me to cover the story. I have to run. Duty calls." She ran out of the room.

"Duty calls?" Clare echoed sarcastically. Marion and Clare were opposite ends of the spectrum. Marion was always talking about more than she knew and Clare always knew more than she said. They had an instinctive disregard for one another. Molly liked them both and was strangely grateful for their mutual animosity.

"Is it true?" Molly asked. She was sure Clare would know.

"What did she tell you?"

"That someone was killed!"

"Molly, it was Nancy." Clare spoke slowly and deliberately.

"No." Molly shook her head. "You're wrong. It's a mistake."

"It's no mistake. They found her body in the parking lot. The police are there and Father Tom anointed the body. I saw her. It's Nancy and she's dead."

Molly slipped on her loafers and headed for the door. Clare grabbed her. "There's nothing you can do."

"Get out of my way." Molly's voice was ice, the anger in her eyes burned cold. Clare let her go. For the only time in her life, Clare Tracey was frightened of and for her friend. Molly headed toward the parking lot, toward the flashing lights and the crowd. Father Tom was there, talking to a man who was loading a black bag into the back of a wagon. In the bag was what was left of Nancy Kiernan. Molly admitted that now. Not because that's what everyone was saying, not because of the pained expression on Father Tom Madden's face, but because now Molly knew. She felt something rip inside and in the gaping wound a terrible reality took hold. Molly watched. She watched the cars drive away. She watched the crowd disperse. She heard the noise around her. She was vaguely aware of the campus returning to normal. But Molly was somewhere else. In a quiet place, at the bottom of the sea or the top of a mountain, surrounded by a mist. Removed. Floating. Suspended.

He saw her, coatless, her hands burrowed in her pockets, her eyes staring straight ahead, her hair covered in snow. She looked more like a Dickensian urchin than a college student. Here was the heartbreak, he thought. The dead were easier than the living. The dead accepted absolution. Their debts were cancelled. Their suffering ended. But the living turned you inside out. Forgive me Father, Love me Father, Counsel me Father. They wanted more than ritual. They created embarrassing situations, posed unanswerable questions. They showed you all the ugly bruises. Their needs were infinite. Their agonies unrelenting. Nancy was easier than Molly, but it was Molly's turn.

He walked toward her. Father Tom brushed the snow from Molly's hair. He spoke to her quietly, the voice of reason--she must return to her dorm, the voice of compassion--he would be there to console her. He took off his jacket and bundled her in it. Finally, the frustration broke through and he shook her violently. "Molly, c'mon, snap out of it! he commanded. Molly stared past him. Then she walked away. She walked out of the gates of St. Anthony University. She walked the two miles of open road into the nearby town. She did not feel the cold. She was oblivious to it. She was aware of the worried glances from the people who passed her on the street, just as she was aware of the Christmas displays in the shop windows. But they were of no consequence. Molly wandered down the side streets of the small town. She noticed a little girl, vainly attempting to dodge snowballs. Molly had been good at that when she was small. She would run and dive and her biggest frustration was that her mittens would ice-ball up, making retaliation impossible.

Long ago, yet the memory was so clear, so unencumbered, so quick to surface. Molly, the little girl, fighting back, giving as good as she got. For a moment, she was there but then it vanished. All day long, certain scenes, certain sounds would trigger memories but then as if they had tried and found it impossible to fill the vacuum, they would retreat. It was late afternoon by the time Molly found her way back to campus. She trudged up to her room, where she peeled off her soaked clothing and climbed into bed. She was fighting for air--strangling. She tossed herself awake. Molly felt the sheets. They were wet with perspiration. She had chills and a fever. Molly changed the sheets and went back to bed. Clare knocked on the door and walked in. "You should lock this, you know," she advised.

"I know," Molly muttered.

"How do you feel?"

"Miserable. I think I've got a cold."

"Really? You should have pneumonia. Where did you go today?"

"I walked to town."

"You walked into town, without boots or a coat?" Clare asked incredulously.

"I had a coat." Molly pointed to Father Tom's jacket, soaked through and drying on the back of her desk chair. Clare was puzzled but unrelenting. Jacket or no jacket, Molly had still been foolish. "Monaghan, you shouldn't be let out without a leash," she stated sternly.

Molly winced. She could never adequately defend herself against Clare's criticism. Clare was so logical, so precise--a typical Math major. It seemed the only times Clare broke the rules the incidents were Molly inspired and Molly orchestrated. Clare was beautiful then. She made the best practical joker, because it was so out of character, so unexpected. There was plenty of the rebel in Clare, though Molly was one of the few people who brought it out.

"Do you want some hot chocolate or something?" Clare asked solicitously.

"Tea," Molly commanded. She enjoyed the attention and she needed the tea.

"Anything else?"

"Na-uh. I have some antibiotics here someplace. Drugs, tea and sleep and I'll be back to my old self."

"In that case, Molly, you might want to reconsider."

"Cute, Clare. Very cute. You do have your moments," Molly mumbled.

"Father Tom called. He sounded very concerned."

"He's very good at that. I think his 'concerned' is pretty good, but his 'very concerned' has to rank among the best," Molly replied sarcastically. She was angry with him. She didn't know why exactly. Molly believed that Father Tom wasn't that fond of Nancy. It wasn't anything he ever said, but then every writer knows that what's unsaid is more important. The truth of feelings are more accurately portrayed in gestures and nuances. When Molly spoke of other friends, Tom would often remark, "She's a great kid, isn't she?" or ""You're fortunate to have so good a friend." Whenever she mentioned Nancy, Tom would just nod. She always had a feeling that he slightly disapproved of her, although Molly couldn't fathom why.

Nancy disliked Father Tom and made no bones about it. She referred to him as Father Narcissus.

"C'mon, Molly, don't you think that's a little unfair, even for you?" Clare was accustomed to Molly's unprovoked sarcasm. "It's not his fault about Nancy."

Whose fault was it? It had to be somebody's. Molly had dealt with death before, but not with fault. Illness, accidents, fate--death just happened: A friend's baby that just stopped breathing. That was all there was to it. End of story. It was terribly sad but it wasn't anyone's fault. Molly's father complaining to her mother about a "little indigestion." Three days later he was buried. "His heart just blew apart." This kind of death was hard, but it was comprehensible. It came with the territory. You bought into it when you left the womb. It wasn't easy, but Molly could accept it. "Unto dust thou shalt return--" every Ash Wednesday in her lifetime helped her with that acceptance. But Nancy's death was different. Nancy's death was personal. It wasn't fate or illness or accident. Nancy's death was indeed somebody's fault. It broke all the rules and violated a fundamental principle.

Clare returned with the tea and some Christmas cookies. "I thought you might like these."

"You're right, as usual."

"Are you going to the Memorial Service?" Clare asked.

Molly tried to grasp the reality. Memorial Service – In Memoriam – Latin for, Oh, God – Latin, the Latin Etymology exam She wanted to care, but she didn't. She'd take the incomplete or the F. It wouldn't be the first time. In Memoriam. Was it in memory of? In memory of Nancy, how could that be? For a moment Molly had no memory. She just went blank. No thought, no memory, no feeling. Nancy's face and voice, her presence they were there, but Molly couldn't summon them.

"Molly? If you want to go, I'll go with you." It was the protective hand that takes yours when you cross the street, the door left ajar, the unsolicited kindness of a friend.

"When?

"Tomorrow afternoon. Nancy's family will be there. They're taking her body home."

"I have to call home. I can't believe I didn't call." She would have to speak the words. She would have to say "Nancy is dead." She knew her mother would ask how? Molly wanted to say there had been an accident, but there had been no accident, no mishap, no tragic, unavoidable, unintentional tragedy. Here, in this place, that Nancy and she had called home, where they had known fun and friendship, achievement and growth. In the black of a winter's night, in the school parking lot, someone had stolen Nancy from them. Molly knew this truth, but she feared saying it.

"You better call now." Clare advised. "Then you should get some sleep. Should I stick around?" Clare knew that it would be a difficult call. Clare was a year younger than Molly, but often acted as a big sister. She was the eldest of four girls and it showed. Molly encouraged her to misbehave and Clare cautioned Molly to be more conscientious. Monaghan and Tracey conversations often sounded like verbal Ping-Pong matches. Most of their friends just sat and watched, like sports fans. Some would utter "Point Tracey" or "Monaghan wins it with an unexpected, obscure reference. Who knew? There were other times though, of serious conversation or simple, uncomplicated dialogue, that cemented their friendship. Clare knew that Molly was hanging on by a gossamer thread. She would be there if that thread broke.

"No, thanks." Molly didn't quite know how she would tell her mother, but she knew she must and when she did she needed to be alone. She knew that others were sad. She wanted to be the person who could think of others first. Molly was not that person. At this moment, she was the little girl lost in the Christmas rush, the condemned man trying to will back the first faint streaks of light, the friend who could not erase the horror of the sight of blood-stained snow.

Clare was leaving when she remembered a message. "Oh, Kevin O'Connor called. He wanted to know if you want to ride with him to Albany for the funeral."

"How did he sound?" She hadn't thought about Kevin, but then she hadn't thought at all. Kevin -- What must he feel about this? Who would be giving him tea and cookies, friendship and comfort. Maybe he was doing shots with some of his buddies. That might work as well.

"He sounded okay, but the word is that he's pretty upset. Besides, the police are having a field day with him. Some detective spent all morning asking him tons of questions about Nancy. I guess a lot of them were personal. The rumor is that Kevin almost decked the guy." Clare said.

"Kevin hit an officer of the law? That's absurd! Did you get that from Marion?"

"Well, they think Kevin killed Nancy. He was the last person anybody saw her with and he does have a bad temper." Molly hated the police at that moment. Nancy was dead and Kevin was their suspect of choice. *Kevin !* If they had done their job right in the first place...almost immediately she felt guilty. Molly didn't blame doctors when patients died or soldiers for the horror of war or the police for crime. It was disheartening though, that they could be this far off base.

"And they think Kevin just happened to have a knife with him on a date? Be real! Kevin O'Connor occasionally loses his temper and yells at somebody. His temper isn't any better or worse than most of the guys around here. He doesn't qualify as a killer. Do they provide him with a motive?"Molly questioned.

"They figure Nancy wouldn't go to bed with him."

"If lust were a motive for murder you wouldn't be able to walk to class around here without tripping over bodies. Anyway, Nancy would have been the suspect, not the victim! Maybe she was right about the police. It's no wonder they never found Louise Porter's killer."

"What are you talking about? Who's Louise Porter?" Clare had not been privy to the story.

"A ghost. Never mind. This whole thing is a nightmare."

Molly drank her tea and ate her cookies and tried to imagine Kevin as a murderer. It didn't work.

"Did the police question anyone else?"

"I guess they spoke with Marion."

"No. Why? Nancy avoided her like the plague." Nancy could not tolerate Marion Schmidt.

Clare smiled impishly. "She volunteered. You know, 'duty calls.'"

Molly shook her head. Clare brought the electric tea kettle from her room so that Molly could replenish her cup without leaving her room.

"Moll," she said hesitatingly, " you haven't cried or anything." Clare sounded as if crying were a legal obligation.

"Yes, I have. I've anythinged." Molly thought that was as good a description as anything else for what she was experiencing.

"You should let go," Clare counseled. "You should cry. Everyone else has. Nancy was one of your best friends and you haven't shown any grief at all. You think you're tougher than you are. You think people expect you to be, but they don't. You'll hold all this in and then you'll just explode." They should never teach Psychology 101. It's a dangerous subject. After three credits, students felt both qualified and compelled to diagnose the immediate world. Why didn't they try to teach wisdom 101-102? What did Clare want as an expression of grief, a weeping and gnashing of teeth? It wasn't Molly's style. Molly couldn't explain. She had been run through. It hurt even to talk. She believed that she might never be whole again.

"Clare, I'm tired, I'm sick and I hurt. Trust me. I am not going to explode. I don't have either the energy or the inclination. All I'm going to do is call home and go to sleep and hope that tomorrow I'll wake up a lot healthier and a little less empty."

"Hello." She heard her mother's voice. Molly tried to speak but her throat tightened., strangling her words.

"Hello?" Molly could picture her mother on the other end of the line. Finally, the words came. "Mama, Nancy's dead." Molly reported Nancy's death to Mrs. Monaghan. She ignored the shock, the grief and concern in her mother's voice. Yes, there would be a memorial service at school. Yes, the funeral would be in Albany. No, Molly didn't know when the funeral would take place. Yes, she would travel to the funeral. No, she wasn't coming home. Yes, she felt safe. Yes, she had a cold and was sad and was going to sleep as soon as she hung up. Yes, she knew her mother loved her and she loved her mother, too.

Molly knew she needed to sleep but wasn't quite sure how that could be achieved. "T'is a consummation devoutly to be wished." When she put her head on the pillow and pulled up the covers, nothing happened. It just felt as if she were riding a roller coaster, speeding down, trying to remind herself to breathe. Would she ever sleep again? Would she ever feel better? Would she ever be whole again?

Molly did sleep and when she woke up she did feel healthier, the cold was pretty much gone but the emptiness remained.

CHAPTER V

The next few days passed in a blur. There were prayers and tears and alcohol and memories. The Kiernans offered their home to Molly and any other St. Anthony student, who came to Albany for the funeral. Mostly, though, the St. Anthony crowd took over a small Howard Johnson's not far from the train station. It would have been too hard to stay at Nancy's. The thought of being surrounded by Nancy's pictures and family and so many memories, seemed masochistic. If Molly thought staying there might have lessened the Kiernans' grief, she would have tried it but she feared that it would just make things harder for them. Molly couldn't offer them any solace. She knew that. The wake and funeral would be difficult enough but Molly did not want to intrude on the Kiernans' mourning.

It wasn't like when Molly's father died. Nancy had stayed with the Monaghans, (although she insisted on sitting with other St. Anthony students during the funeral Mass.) Nancy had been a comfort to Molly and especially to Mrs. Monaghan. They seemed to have a special bond. Sometimes, Molly resented that bond a little. She didn't mind that her mother had emotionally adopted Nancy, but of the two, Molly felt she should be her mother's favorite. Molly's spurts of para-sybling rivalry were always fleeting. Nancy's visits were unadulterated, unequivocal fun. There were fierce pinochle games and late night cookies and coffee. There were lunches and shopping trips and stories.

Over the years, Molly had stayed with the Kiernans as well. They were always gracious to her and friendly. When she was introduced to the Kiernans' friends, it was always as "This is Molly, a school friend of Nancy's." Molly was never "our Molly." to the Kiernans.

"Don't you like Nancy's family?" Molly's mother had asked once, when Molly was less than enthusiastically packing for a weekend with the Kiernans.

"They're very nice." Molly had responded.

"Do you feel out of place there because they have so much more than we have?" Mrs. Monaghan always worried about Molly fitting in. She sometimes acted as if they lived in a shelter. It wasn't that St Anthony was more expensive than other private schools but it had always been a bit of a stretch financially. Molly's brothers went to private Catholic high schools, but without scholarships, they would probably attend the local state or community colleges. Even before Mr. Monaghan died, it had been a challenge. The Monaghans were blue collar people. Mrs. Monaghan had attended a private high school but had never attended college. She had worked in retail until Molly and her brothers came along. Mr. Monaghan had left school for the war. When he returned, he found work in the local steel mill and bartended four nights a week. They were certainly not impoverished but neither were they the country club set. Initially, it had required no small amount of paperwork and a hefty school loan for Molly to attend St. Anthony. Ironically, after Ray Monaghan died, Social Security and other resources made school less costly.

Molly knew there were schools where her economic and social status might be obvious and awkward but St. Anthony University wasn't like that. There were plenty of monied families whose kids attended the University, including a sizable contingent from Long Island, even though they referred to themselves as being from "The City." St Anthony was not the kind of school where there was riding or fencing or even lacross or crew. There were tennis courts somewhere but Molly had never seen a single student in little white shorts or a tennis skirt. The St. Anthony unofficial uniform was comprised primarily of jeans and sweatshirts. Mrs. Monaghan's concern that Molly would suffer from the financial disparity between her and some of the other students, was a waste of emotion. Actually, St. Anthony was fairly diverse financially. In many cases, the students with the most "walk around" money were scholarship students or students from working class families just like Molly's. Money didn't seem to matter much at school. Intelligence, good looks, athletic prowess comprised the currency Molly and her friends recognized.

Molly tried to explain the Kiernans to her mother. "They don't laugh. They are polite and pleasant and it isn't that they aren't witty. It's just that everything is too subtle. They don't really laugh," she complained.

"What do you mean they don't laugh?" Who doesn't laugh, she thought. Perhaps the Kiernans were normal, unlike the Monaghans, who were cursed with Irish "gallows humor." Unlike her husband and most of her friends, Tess Monaghan sometimes lacked to see the humor in tragedies and catastrophies.

"They smile. They don't guffaw, they don't laugh 'til they cry or get the hiccups. I don't think that ever, not once, in the entire history of their dinners did anyone have milk explode through their nose,"

"This is the reason you don't like them? No exploding noses…" Mrs. Monaghan stared in disbelief.

"Yeah, in a way and I *do* like them and my God, their house is beautiful. The guest room, where I stay, looks out over this expanse of lawn that is absolutely breath taking and there's an inground pool and tennis courts. When I'm there, I never have to do dishes or clean or take out garbage and Mama, I know this is hard to believe, but they don't have a single hallway filled with shoes…" The backdoor hallway at the Monaghans' was a minefield of boots and sneakers.

"So you miss the clutter and disgusting dinner incidents? Is that it? Mrs. Monaghan asked, with more than a touch of sarcasm.

"I guess." Molly shrugged.

"That's my girl," Mrs. Monaghan said as she hugged Molly. "Do you think the Kiernans would mind if I went there for the weekend and you stayed here amid the clutter you so love?"

Molly thought of that moment as she watched the funeral procession enter the Church. She wished she had spent more time with the Kiernans. She genuinely did like them and she ached for them now. She felt as if she had robbed them of so much of Nancy's time. Mr. Kiernan looked older, even frail and Molly was grateful that she couldn't see Mrs. Kiernan's face beneath the black veil.

Nancy's brothers and cousins carried her body, in the shiny bronze casket, their grey gloves covered hands strangling the brass handles. Boutonnieres of white roses dressed the button holes of their tailor-made suits. All was clean and somber and correct and the silence and formality screamed louder than a hundred banshees. The altar was crowded with priests, many of them from St. Anthony. Molly wondered if anybody had stayed on campus.

The Church was standing room only. There was an army of Kiernans and plenty of state politicos, the Governor and his entourage, NYS assemblymen and senators. Here and there, a congressman, a judge, various uniforms, police and fire and a sea of black cashmere topcoats, peppered the congregation. Oh so many people, but Molly felt alone and distant. She was cold, perhaps as cold as her friend whom she had bent and kissed goodbye before the coffin closed. Her friend, anointed and eulogized, packed up and ready to be buried. Earth to earth, dust to dust, ashes to ashes. May she and all the faithful departed rest in peace. Amen.

Resquiescat in pacem… More Latin. A dead language for a dead friend, Nancy, at rest. Resting in Peace. That didn't fit.

Molly knelt when required and prayed the familiar words. Normally she would have found comfort in the Mass, in the familiar hymns and prayers, in the solemnity and the sanctity but nothing touched her now. She stood in the long line at Communion and as she walked past Nancy's casket Molly reached out to touch it. "I am here," she thought. "Do you know?" She listened to the gospel: The story of Lazarus. The story of Jesus' friend but no one had killed Lazarus. No one had waited in the cold and dark and took Lazarus from his sisters and his friends. She wondered as the pungent scent of incense pierced the air: What makes someone do that? What amount of fear or anger or revenge would cause someone to kill Nancy? Nancy who had money and power, talent and intelligence…. Nancy whose future was bright with promise and opportunity, who was loved by so many, so very different people. "Look," she thought. "Are you here? Do you see?" Who would do this? Someone who had killed before she thought. Someone who didn't care. Suddenly, Louise Porter seemed very real.to Molly. Before this, she had been a name in a newspaper, an obscure reference, almost something of a nuisance. Molly felt bad about that now. She wondered if that was what Nancy would become -- a homicide victim. Nancy relegated to a name in a file.

Life would go on, of course. All of these people, except for a very few, would mutter "How sad. " and change the subject. Those few, though, of which Molly knew she was one, those few would live in a lessened world.

Molly felt the pressure of her mother's hand on her own. The previous day, the Monaghans had arrived en masse. Mrs. Monaghan had brought baked ham and whiskey to the Kiernans. She had tried to bring them some comfort as well. She had shared Molly's room at the hotel and kept busy acting as a surrogate parent for the other students. She made sure their clothes were cleaned and pressed for the ceremony. She encouraged them to " put something in their stomachs" and to get some sleep the night before the funeral.

Molly could not sleep, even after a liberal amount of alcohol.

"Just close your eyes," her mother advised. She did close her eyes and tried to sleep but she felt like she was falling into an abyss. Her head hurt and she felt like her body was not her own, as if she were trapped in medieval armor, imprisoned, stuck in cement.

She listened to the rhythm of her mother's sleeping breath. Then Molly stood in the darkness. She knew that sleep would not come that night. She was beyond sleep. She was adrift on an endless sea. Part of her remained in a snow covered parking lot. Nancy had been the sister God had neglected to give her. Nancy was her inspiration to achieve, to "swing away," in her writing and her dreams. Gone. Done. Over. There must be something…someway…Nothing. Molly could feel the darkness seep into her very soul.

It had always been there, a tinge of sorrow, a tendency to melancholy. There was always the taste of a tear in the words Molly wrote. She was susceptible to sorrow. When she put a dollar in the panhandler's hand she looked into his red rimmed eyes and saw Greek tragedy. She had been taught to say "There but for the Grace of God go I," but she didn't believe that misery had anything to do with God. She could not believe in a god who plotted and planned, who meted out injustice, a god who allowed children to be molested, who chose some babies to live lives of privilege and others to experience hell. Molly's God did not distribute grace, like get out of jail free cards. Molly believed in luck. Sometimes you could make all the right choices and do all the right things but just happen to be at the wrong place at the wrong time. You could also be at the right place at the right time and that would result in some lucky circumstance. What was the word? Oh yeah-- serendipitous. You could work hard for something and maybe not achieve it but then Molly figured the effort was the prize. It wasn't the grace of God that determined that. It wasn't the grace of God, that made some people addicts and others not.

Molly's version of grace was that God helped you when you needed strength or will power. or comfort. He sustained you in the midst of that which was most difficult. Grace enabled you to do what you needed to do, even though it wasn't possible. Grace helped you to survive, to endure maybe even to excel. It inspired or it sustained, but it didn't determine. Still she murmured, "There but for the grace of God…" because she had been taught to say that and because there was no simple phrase for what she thought or felt. She felt a kinship to the beggar and even to the thief but what pat phrase would explain that?

The night before Nancy's funeral, Molly did not say "There but for the Grace of God…" She did not utter the name of God, nor ask for His Grace. She held the rosary that her grandmother had given her on her First Communion Day, a tiny silver rosary with a Celtic crucifix. It was her grandmother who had taught her the rosary years before second grade. By then Molly not only knew the Mysteries of the Rosary, she could spout off on what days they were to be said: Monday, Thursday and Saturday = Joyful, Tuesday and Friday = Sorrowful and Wednesday and Sunday were for the Glorious. On the morning of her First Communion, Molly's grandmother handed her the silver rosary, saying. "Always keep this close." She had. Of the innumerable possessions Molly lost and misplaced this was not one. She carried it with her in a pocket or purse, everyday.

Molly held it tight in her hand but she did not pray. All words, even those she had uttered all her life, even those she had found comforting and beautiful and which she sometimes worried were so automatic that she may not mean them – all words were hollow and aching. She stood in the darkness, in so much pain, that she had to remind herself to breathe.

The ride back to St. Anthony seemed tortuously slow. "Kevin," Molly said suddenly, "we have to find out who killed Nan." It had occurred to her a little at a time – the way the sky lightens into day. She knew it was probably a bad idea, certainly it could be described as fool hardy and dangerous. That didn't matter. It had taken root.

"Don't be asinine. Everyone's upset by this and you're no exception, but the police have to find Nancy's killer and they will."

"Just like they found Louise Porter's killer?" Molly sneered.

"What are you talking about?" Nancy hadn't told Kevin much about her story. He knew that she was doing an investigative piece on a murder case and had shared that knowledge with the police. They didn't seem that interested. Kevin agreed with their assessment. He was grasping at straws.

"Whoever killed Louise Porter also killed Nancy. I'm sure of it." Molly believed that was the only rational explanation for Nan's murder. There were no serial killers around. Whoever had done it, had targeted her, had waited for her to be alone. There was only one person that could have a credible motive to kill Nancy.

"I'm sure that some madman from twenty years ago didn't just up and decide to make a come-back Talk sense, will you, Molly?" Kevin said in a very old and sensible voice. He sounded more like an insurance agent than Molly's friend and Nancy's lover.

"I am making sense," Molly insisted. "Who would want to hurt Nancy? Listen, the day she died Nancy told me she thought she was close to knowing who killed Louise Porter. *The day she was killed*--doesn't that make sense? Nancy thought she knew. That meant it had to be somebody she had investigated. I think that person killed her."

"She didn't say anything to me when I was with her. Why wouldn't she have said something to me?" Kevin was desperately trying to get past the hurt and the guilt to process what Molly was saying. He already felt responsible for Nancy's death. Why hadn't she gone home with him that night? If she thought she was in danger why didn't she say something?. They had talked for hours – for hours, the last hours of her life.

"Suppose you're right. What difference does that make now? There's no way of finding out what Nancy knew. Somebody ransacked her room the night she was killed. They would have taken any evidence. Did Nancy tell you who she thought did it?" Kevin sounded more angry than cautious.

"No, she didn't tell me whom she suspected, but I have her files." It wasn't her fault that Nancy hadn't confided in him. Besides why was Nancy walking back to the dorm alone? It didn't make sense. Nancy was always so careful, almost paranoid. Why hadn't she gone home with Kevin? Molly knew that Nancy's death wasn't Kevin's fault, but she knew that intellectually, not emotionally. She had read the note a hundred times *"Kevin showed up on my doorstep with an invitation…"*

"You what?" He asked in shock.

"Nancy asked me to look at them. She told me that if after I read them, I thought she should give up the story, she would"

"Wait, was this the favor she asked you to do?" Kevin asked. *Why didn't she ask me?* Why hadn't she told him how serious this story was getting? "When was this again?"

"The day she was killed."

Kevin furrowed his brow. Molly knew he was trying to process this unexpected information. She knew it wasn't fair to spring this on him. ""Life isn't fair." She'd heard that her whole life. Well, if life wasn't fair death certainly couldn't be expected to be.

"Okay. So you didn't read them, right? he asked.

"I haven't been able to." Molly admitted.

."So, get rid of them." Kevin advised. Molly couldn't help but think of her last conversation with Nancy. She wished she had listened better. She wished she had gone to the skellar and joined Kevin and Nancy that night. She knew that she would have to honor her last promise to Nancy. She would have to read her research. No matter how good it sounded, she couldn't just "get rid of" the work that very likely cost Nancy her life.

"Suppose the killer knows that and I'm next on his list?" Molly asked.

Kevin sighed that long "why can't I get through to this person?" sigh. "Look, nobody knows you got anything from Nancy. Even I didn't know. You've been hanging around your friend Marion too long. I'm sure no one's after you."

"Marion's a good kid. She's just shaken up by what's happened."

"Marion is permanently shaken up, but I'm not worried about her. I'm worried about you. If you know anything or have anything Nancy was working on, you need to take it to the police."

"I can't. They won't do anything."

"They can protect you, if in fact, you are in danger." He was about to add, "although I doubt you are," but one glance at Molly's face made him reconsider." "Look, it's possible that Nancy did stumble onto something. If she did and you have it, you have to turn it over."

"Kevin, help me. Please," Molly pleaded.

"I am going to help you. The minute we get back I'm going to call that detective who was so damned interested in me and tell him everything you've just told me.

"You must be fond of attending friend's funerals," Molly muttered.

"Monaghan, you are the most irritating person on the face of this earth. What the hell do you mean by that crack?"

"I mean that it doesn't matter to you how many bodies pile up, as long as you're not involved," Molly stated flatly.

"I wish to Christ I wasn't involved. I wish I had never laid eyes on you or Nancy. I wish I had taken my guidance counselor's advice and gone to some quaint non-sectarian school where the hottest issue on campus was the election of Homecoming Queen." During his tirade Kevin temporarily lost control of the car. They bumped along the side of the road while he regained his composure. Molly waited a few minutes to speak. When she did, she smiled.

"I'm sorry about your incorrect life choices, but you don't have to kill us both because you're in a bad mood."

"Bad mood? Really? Bad mood doesn't adequately describe my present emotional state. If I wake up late or I have a flat tire or I blow a quiz, then I might be in a bad mood. This, Miss Monaghan surpasses that. Furthermore, I am not trying to kill either of us. I am desperately trying to save you. Save, understand, save your *life*. It's much too late for your sanity."

They were silent for awhile. Molly stared out at the miles of snow-covered fields. She tried to understand why she needed to find Nancy's killer. Kevin was probably right. More than likely Molly was not in danger, but if she started looking for a trouble, she was sure to find it. Yet if Louise Porter's ghost had haunted Nancy Kiernan into finding answers, then Nancy could not be expected to let Molly go scot free. The thought that Nancy's murderer would walk away, would be free to live the rest of his life in peace, would turn Molly's future sour. She wasn't after revenge just some sense of justice. Kevin attempted to reason with her again.

"If you're right and you have something that can point to the killer, you could be in big trouble. Even if you're wrong, you're still in trouble. The police are going to be plenty upset with you. There's some law about withholding evidence or something, isn't there?"

"I don't know," Molly said glumly. Although she had completed a pretty comprehensive paper on Freedom of Speech, she was a little rusty on laws relating to homicide.

"Maybe you should find out. The police are very hot under the collar about Nan's death. They questioned me for hours. Did I know Nancy? What was our relationship? Had we ever slept together? Was she a virgin? Was I? Were there any witnesses who could support my statement that Nan was alive when I left her? Was it true I had a bad temper? Had I ever been in a fight? Was I a bed-wetter .. "

"Are you?

"Am I what? he asked, obviously annoyed by the interruption.

"A bed-wetter?"

"I could become one any day now."

"Kevin, please don't go to the police. At least wait until we have something solid."

"WE! When did this turn into we?

A Sleeping Dog

The woman is insane, Kevin thought. She's amazingly dense. He could feel himself being roped in. Women held that power over him. It must be hormonal. They were able to get you to do things you knew you shouldn't. You broke your back carrying things for them, lying through your teeth, saying "Oh, it's not that heavy." You always had to brush the car off, fill the gas tank, change the flat tire. With all their talk of liberation, not one ever insisted on carrying her own luggage. They weaseled you. Managed you.--he way Molly was trying to manipulate him now. My God, she wanted him to corner a killer as a matter of chivalry. The girl was obviously demented. Friend or no friend, woman or no woman, he wasn't taking the hook this time. If she was that determined to do away with herself why couldn't she hang herself in her room or slash her wrists in private? Why did she have to involve him? God help the poor killer she was after. Nancy had complained to Kevin about Molly's stubbornness, how obdurate she could be. If Nancy's killer was smart, he'd take off and never look back. Nancy's killer...What kind of nightmare was this? One night Nancy was beside him and now she was gone.. Nothing made sense and what was absolutely beyond the pale was Molly. Molly, who never got anywhere on time or remembered to bring extra film --Molly was the least careful person that he knew and now she was going after a murderer. No, that was too dangerous, even for Molly, *especially* for Molly.

"How can I help you?" he complained. "How is anyone supposed to help you, when you don't listen? Nancy didn't listen and now she's dead. This isn't some school play or some paperback detective story. This is for real, for keeps. I would have thought today would have brought that message home to you. Both you and Nancy have always been a little crazy, too romantic and sentimental. That's fine as long as you stick to writing poetry and supporting lost causes. It's almost charming. But this is different. There's nothing poetic about Nan's death. It's an enormous, pathetic waste. I can't do anything about that, but I'm certainly not going to help you get yourself killed, too. Molly there isn't much I wouldn't do for you. I'd risk expulsion or arrest and possibly bodily injury. But I won't risk my life and I won't risk yours. Louise Porter died a long time ago. I didn't know her and I don't care about her. Nancy's death…" Suddenly Kevin stopped.

Molly watched him as his grip on the steering wheel tightened. He stared ahead intently. She saw the tell-tale tears fill his eyes. Just as Clare had been concerned about her, Molly had waited for some sign of pain and sorrow from Kevin. Mrs. Monaghan had asked Kevin to sit with them at the funeral, but he had refused. Molly had looked for him in the Church and spied him finally, standing in the back. He seemed unmoved, almost uninterested during the Mass. Now, she saw it. In those few moments, she knew then, that he could not speak, that he dare not open the floodgates of emotion. She realized that Kevin's hold on his emotions was, at best, tenuous. Molly did not want to push him. She didn't know what she would do if Kevin "lost it," When Kevin did speak, it was hardly above a whisper. It was a voice laden with heartbreak and frustration, "Nancy's gone." He said. "It's done. It's over." Molly watched his face redden. She heard his voice get louder. "You can't bring those people back. It's over, do you understand?" Kevin was shouting. now. "Do you?" Molly teared up.

"Don't cry. Crying has no effect on me, none whatsoever. I have five sisters. Believe me I've overdosed on crying. That's the one great thing about sisters, they prepare you for the rest of your life. They break you in early, allow you to build up a tolerance. Here!" He handed Molly a handkerchief, "Blow your nose. I'm immune."

Molly was amazed. She had never seen anyone her age with a handkerchief. Kevin was certainly an enigma.

"Thank you.. Where did you get this? Molly asked.

"What?"

"The hanky. My dad had handkerchiefs like this."

"I think all men's handkerchiefs are pretty much the same. My mother has an aunt who gives me a new handkerchief and a card with money in it every Christmas."

"That is so sweet."

"It is sweet and she's sweet and she'd be very upset if anything happened to me. She'd be unhappy with you if she knew about this conversation. Do you want to stop for coffee or something? Maybe something to eat will make you feel better." Kevin was a great believer in food as a natural consoler.

"Kevin, I just need some time. I know I can figure this out. Then I'll go to the police. I promised Nancy I would look at her notes. As soon as I have something to back up my theory. If I can give them something substantial, then maybe they can nail this guy."

"There isn't any time. By next week everyone will have gone home for Christmas. Until then there are finals and papers to be done. You won't be able to accomplish what you want by then."

"I'll go home for the holiday and simply come back to campus early, before the start of next semester. If I come back right after Christmas, that will give me three weeks. I just need to figure out Nan's notes. I know that I can do it. I just haven't been able to approach it yet. I just need some time."

"That's no good. The dorms won't be open." He could feel the rope tightening around him. What the hell, he thought. What does it cost to listen?

"I thought I could stay at your apartment." Molly explained.

"You could if you wanted, but what will you tell your mother? Won't she be upset that you're staying at my place? You know you're not just staying at a guy's apartment. You're staying with a murder suspect"

"My mother doesn't think that. I told her about the Louise Porter deal. She's really concerned about you. You know that. Do you think she would have hugged you at the wake if she thought you killed Nancy? She'll be grateful that I won't be by myself on campus."

….."And I suppose she'll let you come back early, once she knows what you're planning?"

"I'll explain that I need to go to the library and finish up some work from this semester and start my thesis for graduation. ."

. "She'll buy that?" Kevin asked, amazed by the naivete of the plan.

"She'll buy it. The first reason is that I know I'm getting an incomplete in Latin Etymology and probably Russian History. Secondly, I'm not much of a liar, subsequently I don't lie very often. As a result, my family has created this myth that I'm incapable of it. Besides she'll want to believe it. People tend to believe what they want to believe. My mother, given the choice of believing that I'm working on my writing or doing something dangerous, will choose the former. Most mothers would. The majority of mothers think that their daughters should be married in white." Molly was quite proud of her knowledge of human nature.

"Okay. So your mother will buy it. What do I tell mine?"

"Why do you have to tell yours anything?"

"Because I'm going to stay with you. First, it's probably safer if there are two of us and secondly, it would look very bad for me if yet another close friend ends up dead, particularly if she's staying in my apartment at the time.

"That's a gruesome thought." Molly did not find the role of corpse appealing.

"These are gruesome days." Kevin concluded as he pulled the car into a McDonald's parking lot.

CHAPTER VI

No visions of lollipops danced in Molly's head at Christmas but more than one ghost of Christmas past made an appearance: memories of gifts given and received, memories of Nancy and Kevin and Molly gathering after Christmas Mass at St. Anthony. The gifts they had given to each other last year had all been purchased at a charity bazaar they had attended together. She had given Nancy the knit scarf that Nancy was wearing the day she was killed, the scarf that had mysteriously disappeared. She had given Kevin an Irish cap that was too large and that he never wore. Nancy had given her a book of Irish poems and had given Kevin a beer stein. Kevin gave Nancy a necklace with a tiny pearl. He Molly a photo album. The album was filled with pictures of the three of them with both Nancy's and Molly's poems included. There was a beautiful shot of the altar of the St. Anthony chapel. All of the shots were beautiful. Kevin was good at what he did. He had taught Molly the little she knew about photography, the way to bounce light, when and when not to use a flash, but her pictures were never the same quality as Kevin's. There was love in his photos. As Molly scanned the photos in the album, she realized there was joy as well.

Each picture, every word brought back a memory and razor cut her heart Molly knew she should put the album away. Instead, she let each page wash over her. She looked at the picture of the picnic they had one glorious Spring day at the end of their Freshman year. Molly could feel the sun on her face, the tickle of the grass on her bare legs. On the page across from the picture was a copy of Nancy's handwritten poem:

Picnic

We will need this day,

   Some grey day to come.

         Some cold, collar-up day.

When the wind bites or the rain beats down upon us

         And we will have it

The lilt and light and laughter of this day –

our youth and friendship

         Our Spring, one Spring day

That we will have forever

         No matter how many winters we shall know.

Molly mumbled, "No matter how many winters we shall have." Who could have anticipated this winter? This last winter. There would be another Spring. The snow would melt and the sun would shed its coat and there would be warmth and light again. The grass would grow green on Nancy's grave and the St. Anthony campus would feel its youth again. But for the "we", the three, all seasons had ended. Molly hoped that Kevin had kept copies of the pictures and the poems. She thought maybe she could send some of the pictures and poems to Nancy's parents. When this was over, she could make an album like Kevin's to give to them. If she were still around…

The last picture in the album was a photo of the three of them in caps and gowns. The graduation garb arrived late in their junior year so they could wear it to all the various ceremonies they were required to attend as seniors. Kevin and Nancy wanted to have Christmas cards made from the picture but Molly vetoed the idea. "It's bad luck," she said.

Molly always said things were bad luck. She wouldn't open an umbrella in the house or place a hat on a bed or shoes on a table. She didn't like to plan something as much as a month away, lest something happen and fate intervene. Superstitions. Nancy chided her about them, but maybe Molly had been right. Maybe the picture had been bad luck. There would be no trio of happy graduates now. Nancy was gone and Molly had managed to stack up a pile of Incompletes from the first semester. She really did need to return to campus and make up missed course work.

She wondered how Kevin was doing. She often thought about Kevin. Kevin with his blue-gray eyes and his contagious laughter. Kevin with just the hint of a wave in his auburn hair. She liked Kevin. It made sense, of course, that he and Nancy had gotten together. Molly knew that she would require more. "You're such a romantic." Nancy would chide. Molly preferred to think of herself as an idealist. She thought that Kevin might be similarly afflicted. She sensed beneath his somewhat brusque manner an abundance of caring. He had, after all, gone caroling with them, that one blizzardy day. He had reluctantly given that lost puppy a home until Nancy and Molly found a family that would keep it. The truth was that no matter how loudly he protested and no matter how bitterly he complained, he always came through. He would do it one last time, Molly thought. How ironic, the last favor Kevin would do for Nancy would be to help find her killer.

There was a knock on the door. "Molly, are you awake? Jerry Reardon is downstairs. He wants to talk to you about Nancy." Molly had met Mr. Reardon on more than one occasion. She knew he was a cop and a life-long friend of her parents. She was still confused. It was the day after Christmas, she had slept about four hours and she felt cornered.

"Can I get you some coffee and a Danish, Jerry.?" Mrs. Monaghan was not sure of the protocol. Jerry Reardon had been in her house plenty of times but always socially. This was different.

"Just coffee sounds great, Tess. Please don't fuss."

"She'll be down in a minute. I think she was up most of the night. She's never been an early riser, but since Nancy's death, I don't think she had more than a few hours of sleep. Jerry, have they found out anything? She's talking about going back there, but I don't know. I'm just worried."

"The campus is pretty much closed up, so there's not a lot of information to be had. My understanding is that things will really get going when vacation's over."

"Should I stay in the room? I'm just worried about her."

"It's better if I talk to her alone. I might have to ask questions that would be awkward for her to answer in front of her mother. How about we ask her?"

Molly appeared in a St. Anthony sweatshirt and loose jeans. She had dropped about fifteen pounds since Nancy's death. She had always been a little chunky but she had lost her appetite when she lost her friend.

Jeremiah Reardon, was the head of homicide. He had seen a lot of ugly things. He knew what it was not to sleep at night. He knew what it was like to be haunted. He recognized that in Molly's eyes.

"Hi, Mr. Reardon. I hope you had a nice Christmas."

"Very nice, thanks. I came over to ask you some questions about Nancy Kiernan Is that okay?

Molly wondered if she was a suspect. If they could suspect Kevin, then nobody was off the hook.

" If you want, your Mom can stay. Would you rather have her with us?" She didn't know why exactly, but she didn't want to answer questions in front of her mother. She was a little afraid that her mother might bring up returning to St. Anthony early and then Molly would have to lie to Mr.Reardon. If he didn't ask her exactly when she was returning, she could just not tell him. Just as she could just not tell him that she was staying with Kevin and she could just not tell him about Nancy's notes. Molly knew that these were lies of omission or sins of omission or both. Suddenly, she realized that while she was mentally debating the issue, both her mother and Mr. Reardon were waiting for an answer. Molly shrugged. "It doesn't matter. Is it okay if I have a cup of coffee? I'm a little foggy."

"How about I get the two of you some coffee and then maybe I'll join you for a little bit.

How's that sound? " Mrs. Monaghan suggested.

Molly was trying to grasp the situation.

"Mr. Reardon, I'm sorry, should I call you Lieutenant or Detective or something?" Molly was sitting on the end of the couch next to the Christmas tree. Almost effortlessly, Jerry Reardon had pulled the armchair in next to her.

"It doesn't matter. You can call me Jerry if you want."

Molly smiled. "I can't do that. My father would return from the grave." The Monaghan children were not allowed to call adults by their first names. It was a cardinal rule.

"Well, you've called me Mr. Reardon your whole life. Why don't we stick with that then?"

"Mr. Reardon, shouldn't the local police have interviewed me?

"Normally they would have, but I've been in homicide for a long time and the guy in charge down there is a good friend of mine. I told him I'd be glad to talk with you. It gives me an excuse to visit with you and your mom and get paid for it." His smile was warm and somehow reassuring.

"You don't mind, do you?"

"No. I kind of thought my mother might have called you anyway."

"Yeah." He smiled. She was her mother's daughter. "You caught us. The truth is that when your friend was killed, your mom called me right away. I figured they would want to talk to you so I called the police department down there and asked if it would be okay if I handled things on this end. They were fine with it and said they'd keep me updated on the investigation." he said. Then he added, "That way, of course, I can report to your mother.

"I was kind of surprised that the homicide detective that came to campus didn't interview me. Although he really didn't talk to many people. He seemed exclusively focused on Kevin."

"Kevin O'Connor?" Mr. Reardon had taken a small notebook out of his pocket and was checking something he had already written."

"Kevin was Nancy's boyfriend, right?"

"Yes. Well …sort of."

"Sort of?"

"I mean, yes. They were involved, but they were more friends than a couple. Does that make sense?"

"Were they involved sexually?" he asked, matter-of-factly.

"Yes." She could feel the heat rise in her face. At school, sex was no big deal. There was a fair amount of what some people referred to as casual sex. Molly guessed there may have been a little less "active socialization" than at most places where you had a cluster of late teens and early twenties. The Franciscan philosophy of love that the university espoused was more aesthetic than physical.

"Were they together for a long time, do you know?"

Mrs. Monaghan brought in two big Christmas Mugs with coffee.

"You know, Kate, maybe I could use a pastry or something.. Do you have anything apple?

"I do. Molly would you like something?"

"Just the coffee. Thanks."

Molly had always liked Mr. Reardon, but she especially appreciated his attempt at discretion at that moment. "It's okay. Mr. Reardon." Molly confided. "Mama probably knows more about Nancy than I do. They've had lots of late night/early morning talks."

"I should have known. What about you? Is there anything you haven't shared and would prefer that your mother not know?"

"If you mean sex, unfortunately not. I think my mother would actually be okay with a little romance in my life but it just hasn't happened." Molly was usually disappointed about the total void of eroticism in her life, but right at this moment. she was grateful. She was glad not to have to explain any personal sexual relationships to Mr. Reardon. It was awkward enough explaining Kevin and Nancy's. It was true, Molly thought that her mother would probably be fine about it but her father wouldn't have been. Mr. Reardon, cop or no cop, man of the world or not, was of the same ilk as her dad.

" I've been thinking about the time thing with Kevin and Nancy and it seems like the sex aspect of it started about last year around Thanksgiving or a little before."

"How did you feel about that?"

"Pardon me?" Of course, Molly had been affected by the sexual involvement of Kevin and Nancy. She had feared that it would end badly, that she might lose one or both of her friends

"I don't know. On some level, I was happy for them but I was worried one or both of them. would get hurt. I was afraid that things might get nasty. Over four years, I've seen that happen a lot. Really good friends get together and are a hot item for two or three months. Then they split up and things get awkward and difficult. Sometimes after a while though, it can get better but it's never the way it was. Friendships get broken. I was afraid of that, I guess." Molly confessed.

"Did that happen?" Mr. .Reardon inquired.

"No. That's what I meant by sort of. I think in the beginning Nancy was really in love with Kevin. It was like she had this epiphany. They were friends. Then she kind of fell in love with him and then, it just sort of dissipated. Kevin's a great guy and a terrific friend, but he's not Don Juan, you know. For Kevin, even at the beginning, he just didn't seem that into it. There wasn't the kind of passion. I think the sex was more convenient – I mean, I don't know what the actual sex was like, but there wasn't a lot of flirting or anything. I guess because they never seemed to be that intense. It was comfortable"

"Besides being afraid it would end your friendships, did you have any other feelings when they got together?"

"I felt a little left out." Molly was ashamed to admit it. "You know at first, when they'd be talking about where to go or what to do on one of their dates, I'd feel excluded. That part of it didn't last that long. Actually. if either of them had happened to fall in love with somebody else, then we'd likely have seen a lot less of him or her. That's pretty normal. It wasn't like we didn't have other friends, different circles. If Kevin and Nancy were out together, I wasn't sitting home feeling lonely. Friendships sometimes have to change to survive."

...."Were they as philosophical about change? Did either of them get involved with someone else? Could Kevin have been jealous?

"Both of them dated other people occasionally. Look, I don't want you to think that Nancy was promiscuous or anything. She never really was serious about anybody else. As far as I know she wasn't ever intimate with anyone else. Both Kevin and Nancy were interested in very different careers and neither wanted to spend the rest of their lives with one another. They just really enjoyed spending time together. Does that make sense?"

"It doesn't to me, Molly. I think it may be generational It seems a little too laid back for my taste."

"It isn't that we're some kind of free love cult." Molly thought for somebody who was hoping to earn her living working with words, she was doing a deplorable job explaining this. She was concerned that Mr. Reardon would think that Nancy and Kevin and she were perverts or deviants or just hippie types. "You know, it was never a 'fair field no foul kind of deal'. I don't want you to think we're morally bereft. We care about a lot of stuff. We're passionate about writing and photography and politics. I guess this just sounds weird. Mr. Reardon, I just need you to believe that there's no way Kevin would have hurt Nancy. It's absurd. I've known Kevin for almost four years. He wouldn't hurt anyone."

"Well, I've been in this business a long time and I still can be surprised. The one thing I can tell you for sure is you *never* know." How many times had the boyfriend or husband who "couldn't be" the murderer, ended up the guilty party? In the Kiernan case, he locals liked the boyfriend for it. The problem was it didn't feel right. Besides, some students had seen Kevin drive off and Nancy head toward her dorm. Although what students were doing roaming around the campus all hours of the night was beyond him.. Just because he drove away didn't mean that he couldn't have come back and killed her, but frankly, from what Molly was saying, the guy didn't sound that energetic. Reardon would have liked to have pinned it on this guy just for being such a schmuck. In his day you walked the girl to her door. She didn't see you safely home and then walk home in the dark alone.

One thing for certain, Jerry didn't like the idea that Ray Monaghan's kid was involved in this. A Catholic campus – Jesus, what a mess. If it wasn't the boyfriend, then who could it be? Was there some lunatic running around? Could Molly or the other female students also be in danger?

"I know, about this, I know for sure." Molly said vehemently. "I also know that if Nancy hadn't decided to investigate the murder of Louise Porter, she'd be alive right now and we wouldn't be having this conversation."

"Who's Louise Porter?" he asked.

Molly took a long drink of coffee. "You're kidding. Really? Mr. Reardon, are you saying they're not even talking about Louise Porter? It's unbelievable!"

Unlike the local police, Jerry Reardon was very interested in Nancy's investigation. It made sense to him that Nancy may have made somebody very nervous.

"So are you saying that your friend, Nancy was investigating an open murder case? "He was stunned.

"I guess. It happened twenty years ago. I think the police had kind of given up on it."

"It might seem that way but a murder case has no statute of limitation. Over time, it might become what we call a cold case, but we never give up on it."

"Oh, I didn't know." Molly said pretending she had been wrong. Molly was certain the local police had given up on Louise's murder, regardless of what Mr. Reardon said. She was sure of it, regardless of Mr. Reardon's contention.

"That seems pretty risky. Do you know why she was interested in this?

Molly thought she did, but once again, she was afraid that her explanation would do an injustice to Nancy. "It was for a Journalism class, Investigative Reporting. Nancy was a terrific student. She looked at old town papers to see if there was anything interesting and she found the murder."

"Who knew about it, about her investigation?

"I don't know. I did. I think Kevin did and our Journalism professor. I guess anybody she interviewed. The local police knew." Molly thought suddenly that because they knew, that must be why they're not telling anybody. She could tell by Mr. Reardon's face that he was thinking they should have stopped her.

"Are you sure of that."

"Yes, sir." She wasn't going to tell Mr. Reardon how she knew. She was glad he was interested in Louise Porter's murder. Nonetheless, Molly didn't share with him that she had Nancy's files or that she was returning early to continue Nancy's work. She wasn't sure why. She trusted Mr. Reardon, but he wasn't officially in charge of Nancy's murder investigation and she also feared that he might convince Mrs. Monaghan to keep her home.

Mrs. Monaghan joined them and they talked a little more about Nancy. Mr. Reardon took copious notes. He asked about the "God squad." "Who were they? What did they do? Were they upset with Nancy "falling away" from the group? Could they have marked her as evil? Molly told him all she knew, including that she considered the God Squad weird but not dangerous.

"What about this Brother Germaine? Reardon asked.

"I don't know much. He spent some time in France. I think that's where he got into the movement"

"And this movement is Catholic? This Brother Germaine, the school's okay with this?" He looked skeptical.

Molly tried to explain, but she wasn't precisely sure about any of it. She knew that Jerry Reardon and her parents were traditional in their Catholicism. Her father wasn't even that fond of English as opposed to Latin. Molly, herself was in many ways singularly conservative for her age.

"I don't know that much about the whole thing. It's based, I guess on the seven gifts of the Holy Ghost. They have these charisms. I think that's what they're called. They include speaking in tongues, you know, like the Apostles on Pentecost. Some people see visions and at meetings some people fall on the floor and get "slain by the Spirit.""

Jerry Reardon was writing furiously.

"Slain by the Spirit? Is that a kind of exorcism?" he asked.

"Again, I'm not sure. I was never a member. It might be kind of like when the Bishop slaps you at Confirmation. Brother Germaine bops them on the head before they fall down."

Reardon looked shocked. "He hits them?"

"It's just with the heel of his hand on their forehead. He doesn't deck them or knock them out or anything." Molly drank her now lukewarm coffee. She wished she knew more, that she had paid more attention to Nancy when she had explained it all. She was afraid of the image she was providing of her best friend. He didn't know Nancy. He hadn't seen how she had been moved by the faith of the Charismatics, by the sheer emotion of the movement. Molly was unnerved by what she considered the "crowd mentality" of the movement, the near hysteria of their gatherings. She feared she would see them some night running through the campus with torches looking for witches. Molly asked Father Tom about it. He had given her some of the theological background and had told her not to worry. He said, more or less, that Nancy would probably tire of it and that he doubted that the Charismatics were violent. Molly believed that.

"I think Brother Germaine's kind of spooky, but I don't believe he'd ever hurt anyone. He definitely believes in hellfire. I can't imagine he would ever risk that."

It was a long morning, After several cups of coffee, a ham sandwich and half-a dozen tiny fruit Danish, Mr. Reardon said goodbye. He told Molly that she could expect to have a visit from the local police after the beginning of second semester. He handed Molly a business card and wrote a phone number in ink on the back of the card. "This is my own number." he said. "Call me anytime If you're nervous about anything or you think you remember something important – Call. Promise." He put his hand on her shoulder. "Try to get some rest while you're home." he advised.

"Sure. Mr. Reardon, thanks. Safe home."

He hesitated at the door and added, as if it were an afterthought, "Molly, I know you're friends with this O'Connor guy and you're convinced he's not involved in this, but I want you to listen to me. When you go back to school, you just finish up your courses and keep your distance from Mr. O'Connor and the God Squad or anybody else who could be remotely involved in Nancy's death. You wouldn't be a Monaghan if you weren't stubborn, but I don't expect you to be stupid. We'll find out who killed your friend. You need to make sure we don't have any other homicides to investigate."

Molly had been right. Jerry Reardon would not have approved of her plan. "Thanks again, Mr. Reardon. Safe home"

Jeremiah Aloysius Reardon was not a happy man. Molly was not going to be smart. Well, there were three weeks before the next semester started. She'd be safe until then. He might be able to take a little road trip before the second semester began. This Louise Porter thing might well be the key. He wondered why his sheriff friend hadn't mentioned that. He shook his head, lit a cigar and turned on the ignition.

He looked over his notes. Jerry Reardon had known Molly since she was a baby, but even if she had been a stranger he would have known something was amiss. Molly was not being completely forthright. Maybe she had a crush on the boyfriend. Maybe she had a crush on the victim. For sure she was holding something back. He hoped that she was right about this O'Connor character and that she wasn't in any danger. He had a couple active cases on his desk right now. Still, he would have to keep an eye on this. "Hell of a thing," he muttered as he put his ten year old Lincoln into gear. Even as he pulled out of the driveway, Molly was packing her bag.

Despite Molly's great understanding of human nature, she had seriously underrated her mother's opposition to an early return to the University. In addition, she had expected her mother to back Molly in her staunch support of Kevin. Although Mrs. Monaghan told Jerry Reardon that she was sure that Kevin was innocent, she wasn't nearly as enthusiastic in his defense as Molly anticipated. As a result, Molly felt compelled to lie about where she was staying and with whom.

Finally, the combination of first semester incompletes and the prospect of Molly working on her thesis won the day. Success was the result less of Molly's powers of persuasion than Mrs. Monaghan's personal philosophy. Tess Monaghan believed in action. "Get up and get going" was her lifelong motto. A week after she buried her husband of twenty-seven years, Tess was back at work. All the thank you notes had been mailed and .all the necessary paperwork had been signed, sealed and delivered. It wasn't that she was callous or that she was not grieving. Molly knew her mother was heart-broken. She saw it in her mother's face at every dinner time. Mrs. Monaghan would look across the table at where Ray always sat and her expression conveyed pain and loss in stark certitude. Molly heard it in her mother's voice, when she would touch Molly's shoulder "You are so like him." In those moments Molly thought of her mother as an open wound.

Although, she may have seemed so to some Tess Monaghan was far from cold or even stoic. She was driven. She feared "giving into" grief or illness. When another woman might have taken a valium to relax, Mrs. Monaghan would work for three hours in her garden. When she had a bout with insomnia after Ray's death, she just threw herself into her work, so that she was so exhausted her body refused not to sleep. When she was worried or sad or anxious, she spent hours doing laundry or cleaning or volunteering.

Nancy's death had been an unexpected blow to the Monaghans. Tess had comforted and consoled and cooked. By Christmas Eve all the presents were wrapped and the tree was decorated and even the Christmas cookies were baked and frosted. Seasonal traditions were scrupulously observed, but the Monaghans were simply going through the motions. Even those were difficult for Molly.

Mrs. Monaghan was concerned about Molly's lack of appetite and her penchant for isolation. In truth, she had always worried that she would lose Molly to depression. As much as Tess worked through every emotional crisis, so that no melancholy could catch her and "grab hold of her", Molly seemed to just stand there and take it. Worse than that, she seemed to attract sorrow and embrace misery. Tess' father, whom Tess adored and whom Molly "was the spit of" had been like that. Tess and her siblings always blamed "the drink" for the sorrow that shrouded their father. With Molly, she had seen it at first glance. "My God, she thought, as she nursed her only girl, she has my father's eyes, those lovely, sad eyes." Thus, when Molly said she needed to catch up on her work and throw herself into her studies, however un-Molly it seemed, Tess thought it was an answer to her prayers.

""Your sister needs time and she needs to be busy." she explained to other family members when they expressed apprehension. "Time heals all wounds." her mother advised Molly, but Molly wanted something more than healing from time. She wanted answers.

CHAPTER VII

Kevin met her at the bus station. They went to his apartment and sat on the over-sized, over-used once green velvet couch. They split a six-pack of beer and a pound of memories. Between them there existed an easiness, a familiarity that marks the best of friendships. They could admit faults. They could cherish qualities. They could come home to each other. Kevin's was a one-bedroom apartment with a minute kitchen and bath. The living room could be located beneath mountains of Kevin's camera equipment and books. Several of the items that cluttered the apartment were of an unknown or unrecognizable origin.

The landlord owned a camera-shop on the main floor of the building and Kevin worked there on a part-time basis. Most of the students at St. Anthony considered Kevin's position an enviable one. He was allowed free use of the darkroom, the equipment, chemicals and paper supply of the shop. In addition, he lived rent-free in the upstairs apartment. Because the owner had been impressed with Kevin's work, he gave Kevin a small weekly stipend. Molly figured Kevin deserved it, but Kevin was of the opinion that fate had smiled upon him.

A Sleeping Dog

It was Kevin's idea to set up a schedule for the investigation. He would need some time to work in the shop. As long as he was back early from vacation it made sense to try and improve his finances. His motives were more than monetary. If anybody were watching, his working would provide a valid reason for returning early from vacation. At least it would provide Kevin with an acceptable excuse. Molly would be harder. Nobody but Molly's mother would fall for that line about working on a paper. Molly figured she and Kevin could pretend to be lovers. Because of the low key relationship between Nancy and Kevin, most people were not aware of it. Even if they knew, it wouldn't seem strange for Molly to seek out Kevin for solace and security. They were used to seeing Kevin and Nancy and Molly together. Now it would look as if Kevin had to come back to work and Molly came back early to stay with him. Why not appear as just another "campus couple?" It was the perfect cover. Well, it was a cover anyway. If Nancy's killer suspected anything, maybe this would convince him not to worry. He might easily conclude that they were too busy with one another to be too much of a threat to him. Having established a cover story, they could proceed with the investigation.

Next, they would need to compile a list of suspects, people who were on or around campus at the time of both Louise Porter's and Nancy Kiernan's murder. It was important to concentrate on the Porter killing.

That would lead to solving Nancy's murder. There were lists to compile, to be referenced and cross-referenced. Kevin and Molly would need to go through old year books and newspapers. There were clues there that Nan had only hinted at in her notes. There were Nancy's files, of course, but they were almost impossible to decipher. Nan had used some kind of code. Molly had studied the system for several hours, but couldn't crack it. Maybe Kevin could. He was better at things like that. (He could, after all, complete the Sunday Times crossword.) It was a monumental task, but after a few beers and a little organization, it seemed merely formidable.

"It can be done." Molly assured herself as she burrowed into the couch cushions. (Kevin and Molly would take turns sleeping on the sofa. It was the only fair sleeping arrangement. Molly would have insisted upon it, but unfortunately argue the point. She took the couch for the first night.) "We'll be able to do it," she tried to convince herself, but there were nagging doubts. They were two amateur detectives, miles out of their league. Even fictional mysteries were solved by professional detectives. In literature, everything was clear-cut and rational. There were always plenty of clues, so that an astute reader often guessed the guilty party long before he was revealed. The other thing was that the protagonist not only solved the crime but lived to tell about it.

A Sleeping Dog

When Molly was in high school her English essay questions would begin, "In literature as in life…" Molly always argued that literature and life weren't interchangeable. She thought that held for the mystery genre as well as science fiction. This might be particularly true in the present circumstances.

What kind of chance did she and Kevin really have? She could stop now and instead actually work to complete her first semester courses and begin her thesis. She could expend her energy toward graduating with her class and beginning a life outside of St. Anthony, free of fear and grief. Reason demanded that she give up the project. Reason makes you old, she argued. Ah, but old is better than dead, a tiny voice replied.

"Molly, wake up." Kevin was standing over her, shaking her.

"What?" Molly rubbed the sleep from her eyes and tried to focus. Kevin was standing in fromt of the couch, in his boxer shorts, his hair standing straight up on the top of his head. He looked like a rooster. Kind of a cute rooster, though.

"Molly, you were screaming." he said shakily.

"Not me." Molly retorted. "I don't scream, I don't giggle and I don't faint. It's in my contract. I don't even talk in my sleep."

"You didn't talk. You cried. You sounded as if you were being tortured."

"I'm sorry, Kevin. It was a bad dream, that's all." Molly had always had graphic dreams. She would often dream in color, action dreams with complicated plots. Sometimes she would have dreams within dreams, where she explained a dream to someone in a dream. Molly often had pleasant dreams, sweet dreams as her mother often wished her. But her dreams could also portend impending disaster or calamity. Before her father's death, she had dreamt of being attacked by a strange bird, an augur of misfortune. She had not slept much since Nancy's death and was grateful for that because when she did her dreams were not sweet.

"Well since I'm already awake, did you want to talk about it?" He was concerned and Molly appreciated concern. She had to be careful. She had been babied all her life - pampered and fussed over. She had to work hard to face the harsh realities of life without smothering herself in the generous sympathy of family and friends.

"Will that exorcise all the demons?" Molly asked. It was wonderful - that cushion of sympathy - and it was tempting. How often in her life had she fallen into it, discovering how it became a velvet trap?

"Demons, huh? I don't know. Demons aren't exactly my specialty, but I think sometimes it helps to talk about things. Dreams can tell you a lot, both good and bad dreams. Besides, it could be interesting - any whips, chains or perhaps a selection of leather goods involved?" She laughed. Kevin could always make people laugh. That was one of his greatest attributes. It wasn't as though he tried - he never told jokes or terribly funny stories. He simply said things with a certain suggestive quality and then treated his audience to a sort of half-smile that was all mischief.

"Negative. Anyway what makes you assume that I would necessarily categorize that kind of dream as bad?" Molly never had erotic dreams, but she was sure if she did, she would chalk it up as overactive hormones and enjoy them. One night, after she had seen her first ballet., it gave her a whole new appreciation for men in tights. She had trouble sleeping that night, but she couldn't remember any dream. It wasn't fair really, it was as if she had an innate censor.

"Just an educated guess" Kevin said with a smirk. "C'mon, you can tell me. Any small animals, large animals, reptiles?" Kevin was on a roll now. For a moment Molly wanted to tell him that he was right and that in the dream she was hopelessly enamored of a Great Dane, but was being pursued instead by his friend a Bull Terrier. It was a fleeting temptation.

He probably wouldn't be shocked anyway. Knowing Kevin he'd just shake his head and mumble something about Freud. Molly opted for the truth.

"Negative. Really, it's not very interesting." She confessed. "If you really want me to tell you about it, I will. I'm afraid you're going to be devastatingly disappointed."

"How do you know?"

"Just an educated guess. Should I make tea or coffee or hot chocolate or something?" Why was it that even when guys were comforting you, they never offered to make the tea? They might offer you a beer, but then they didn't have to brew that.

"The hot chocolate sounds like a good idea. I suppose I should put some jeans on.

"Suit yourself, Kevin. I have seen men in their underwear before." Molly had seen her father and her brothers in their underwear, but seeing Kevin in his made her a little uncomfortable. She would, however, rather die than admit that.

"Well, no wonder you have such disturbing dreams. Perhaps you're disappointed I woke you." Kevin muttered as he headed toward the bedroom. Molly bundled up in her robe and headed to the kitchen. Molly didn't really mind making the hot chocolate. It gave her something to do, something productive and something that would keep her from going back to sleep. It was comfortable padding around Kevin's kitchen in her slippers.

Nothing in Kevin's kitchen matched. The stove was olive green and the refrigerator was yellow. The cupboards were wooden with glass windows. A previous tenant had painted the wood to match the refrigerator. The old wooden kitchen table sat in a recess below the kitchen window. Its top was white porcelain with black sailboats painted on it. It reminded her of the kitchen table at her grandmother's house. When she was little Molly would sit at that kitchen table and trace the design with her fingers. Her grandmother's table top had blue houses painted on it. She used to imagine that there were little people in those houses and at night, when everyone was asleep they came out of the houses and skated across the table. Sometimes Molly would notice small scratches on the table and attribute them to the miniature skaters.

Molly poured the hot chocolate into two giant mugs, stirred, then tapped the spoon on the bottom of each one. She had always loved the click the spoon made when she stirred hot chocolate. It was a different sound than when she stirred tea or coffee. She didn't know why, but it always made her feel cozy. Hot chocolate for winter nights and storms, ginger ale for illness, alcohol for big events and "get togethers" and coffee all day everyday – that was Molly's beverage rule.

"It's always the same". Molly said as she sat, her hands hugging the steaming mug.. "I've been having pretty much the same dream since the day Nancy was killed. In the dream, I'm walking. It's as if the city is being evacuated and everyone is crowded together pushing forward. They're all walking as fast as possible, but it's really slow-going because of the traffic. Everyone seems calm, but there's this prevailing sense of panic. My family is there, somewhere in the crowd, but they're walking ahead of me. I can see them but I don't seem to be able to catch up with them. I lose sight of them and I panic a little. Then I see them and I think, why don't I call to them? I think if they looked back they would see me. If I can see them why can't they see me? .Anyway, as I'm trying to push through the crowd to get to them, I see this old steel mill. I notice there's a dirt path beside the mill and the road leads out into the river.. I can see my family crossing the bridge up ahead. Everyone seems anxious to cross the bridge, to get away. Then I look out toward the water and I see someone standing far out on the break wall. I realize that it's Nancy and I call to her, but she doesn't seem to hear me. So I start to walk out to her. I keep thinking it can't be Nancy. She's dead, but there's no mistaking her.. The further I walk, the deeper the water gets and I know I have to turn around and go back. I know I have to join my family and escape, but instead I just keep going. I don't see Nancy anymore. I don't see anyone. I hear people calling to me from the shore, but I can't go back. I know the water is going to drown me and I want to live, but it's as if my body just ignores me. It gets darker and darker until I can't see anything. It's as if I've entered some secret chamber, some dark forbidden place. I feel light, not lamplight, lightweight., weightless and I'm only faintly aware of the water pouring over me. I don't hear anything but my heart beat and that's racing. It's as if my body were paralyzed, yet my mind keeps working. It keeps warning me that I am dying and I'm fighting it, but it's winning. Then I wake up and my chest is pounding and my body feels like I've just completed the New York Marathon. I have to take shallow breaths to keep the pain to a minimum. I can figure the dream out, but I can't stop dreaming it."

"You've figured all that out?" Kevin wasn't smiling anymore.

"It's my subconscious saying it's frightened," Molly said in a half-whisper.

"You're subconscious sounds like it's positively scared to death." Kevin surmised.

"It's more than my subconscious. It's all of me. Kevin, I'm really scared. I'm totally and unequivocally terrified." Molly was shocked by the frankness, the open vulnerability of her admission. Molly always tried to appear tough because basically she believed she wasn't. She had been raised with her brothers, in a working class neighborhood. She played hard and was given no quarter for her gender. (To her credit she asked none.) Molly suffered so many cuts and bruises that her father shook his head in dismay and stated. "I thought when I had a girl I wouldn't have to worry about this. Why can't you play with your doll house? You're worse than your brothers."

At an early age Molly had determined that life could be very challenging, but that those who survived, who somehow found a way to endure the hardships and celebrate the victories - were those who just kept going. Maybe she was living according to cliches, but Molly believed that if you admitted even to yourself how deeply you felt things - if you articulated the immense pain or joy - or terror - you'd be overwhelmed and very possibly you could never pick yourself up and keep moving.

It surprised her that suddenly she could say to Kevin "I'm terrified." Until this moment, she had never admitted it to herself. Kevin took a long drink of the no longer hot chocolate and leaned back on the couch. Molly was curled up beside him like a cat..

"Molly, can you forget about this? Could you just grieve for Nancy like everyone else and go on with your life?" he asked gently.

"No." She was certain of that. She wanted to grieve. She wanted to return to life the way it had been, but that life was gone. Someone had stolen it. She was afraid and she didn't want to be afraid, but there didn't seem to be a way not to be. If Nancy's murder went unsolved, Molly would never stop looking over her shoulder. She'd be haunted forever by Nancy and by Louise Porter and by her own cowardice. Maybe she wouldn't be able to solve it, but she would have to try. She had to honor a promise, spoken in a dining hall and the unspoken pledge of a friend and sister.

"Okay," Kevin said, "then I'm going to tell you something and you're going to believe it. I wasn't in favor of this. I still think it's decidedly foolish, but as long as I'm committed to it, that's it. I'll see you through it. We're going to get this person. It's not going to be the other way around. Understand? I'm going to be there with you and we're going to succeed. Don't make yourself crazy. I won't let anything happen to you. You've got to trust me, to believe what I'm saying to you. Maybe then there won't be any more of your dreams. I have dreams too. I keep thinking that if I had made Nancy come home with me that night or if I had just gotten off my ass and walked her to the dorm, she might still be alive. If I had known, I would have protected her. I can't do anything about that, but I can protect you and I will." Kevin looked so serious, so determined, so credible. She studied him for a moment. Yes, he could protect her. He was six-feet, give or take a smidgeon and he weighed about a hundred-ninety pounds. He had muscles where he should have them, but more importantly, he had emotions. If Kevin said he wouldn't let anything happen to her, then nothing would. She could believe him, feel safe with him.

Molly wished that he would embrace her. Just at that moment, she wanted all the dime-store romance she so severely criticized. Why couldn't they share a night of wild abandon? Why not Kevin who was strong and good and probably a wonderful lover? Why not Kevin for an evening of mad-passion? Because, she concluded, with Kevin, it would be more like reckless endangerment than wild abandon. Besides her conscience was on high alert, Kevin was her friend. He had been Nancy's lover. There was something incestuous about sleeping with your best friend's bed-partner-- even if your best friend was dead or maybe because she was dead. No, Kevin would have to be someone else's tall, dark stranger. For Molly, he would have to remain Kevin, reliable, responsible and please God, courageous Kevin.

Molly finally succumbed to sleep. In his room, Kevin did not. He tossed and turned and feared that he was making a mistake. What he had told Molly was true. He had been plagued by "If onlys…" He knew if they could uncover Nancy's killer, then that would be good for him.

For one thing, he'd be off the hook for Nancy's murder. He knew that he was innocent, but that didn't mean they wouldn't still come after him. He was sure that some of the people in jail were innocent. Innocence didn't necessarily assure acquittal. Even if they never arrested him, it didn't mean that there wouldn't always be a shadow of doubt. Kevin hated the idea that twenty years from now, instead of being remembered as the guy who took great pictures or the yearbook editor, that he would be the guy who may have gotten away with murder. It wasn't just here either. What happens ten year from now, when he is asking some woman to be Mrs. O'Connor? "Darling, by the way, I should probably tell you that a number of people suspect that I killed my college girlfriend." That would certainly add to the romance.

The best thing would be for the police to find Nancy's murderer. So what if they hadn't solved Louise Porter's death. That was twenty years ago. They have avenues of discovery now that they didn't have then. Besides if money talked, the Kiernan name roared. Where were all the big guns? Was it possible that the Kiernan's would let Nancy's death go unsolved? He was sure it was only a matter of time before the FBI and maybe private investigators were knocking at his door, turning his life inside out. Still, wouldn't they for sure find this guy? If he could be certain of that, he could convince Molly to trust the cops. The problem was Kevin wasn't sure. It had been weeks since Nancy's murder and he hadn't seen or heard from the police, local or otherwise since the morning of her death. Now Molly had moved in with him. What if he had murdered Nancy? They hadn't even tried to warn Molly.

Maybe they were watching him. If that were true, then maybe Molly and he were safer than he supposed. Maybe. Anyway, it didn't matter, regardless of the risk. Molly wouldn't change her mind. In a way he respected that. Molly was indomitable of spirit. There was the real possibility though, that both Molly and he could lose their lives. He said he would protect her, but how? Molly's nightmares were at night, but everyday had become a nightmare for Kevin.

He had loved Nancy. He could admit that now. He missed her. Kevin knew that Nancy didn't love him, not in a romantic sense. What if she were just protecting herself, just the way he did, by not committing to a real relationship? What if they had a shot at all that romantic nonsense that filled books and television specials and they had tossed it away? Did they ignore something real to remain cool? Stupid. He was stupid and he was faithfully remaining stupid by adding regrets to the already burdensome pile of "Why didn't I? s that now plagued him.. It didn't matter. Molly was right. If Nancy had died in an accident or suffered an illness, then both she and Kevin could have survived Nancy's death with just normal grief and sorrow. It was Nancy's murder that had sealed their future. If they didn't find this guy…No, they had to find him. He couldn't get away with this. If they figured it out…No, *when* they figured it out, he would go to the police. Then he could graduate and go away and never look back. Molly would be free, too.

Kevin prayed. He had not prayed in a long time. He hadn't experienced a crisis in faith. He had no strong objections to the Church or any real questioning of her teachings. He just stopped. He could remember, as a kid, after his bath, in his PJs, his hair still damp, combed back off his face, he knelt: "As I lay me down to sleep…" Then, he stopped kneeling, but he still prayed – An Act of Contrition every night and the morning offering (pasted in the corner of the bathroom mirror) every morning. His Freshman year at St. Anthony, he occasionally attended Sunday Mass. Then he just stopped. He got busy with the paper and the yearbook, with writing and mostly with photography and he didn't pray anymore. It didn't mean anything. He did it by rote. He wondered if he ever meant it. There was a time when he believed in heaven and hell. Kevin could remember: "Who made you? God made me. God made me to know love and serve Him in this world and be with Him in the next.

Right. He had been an altar boy. He had learned the Latin, something about washing, I go to the altar to wash, lavabo est? Agnus Dei, Lamb of God. He had rung the bells. Then there was the change to English. Still bits and pieces of the Latin floated on the periphery of memory. He still served, though it wasn't the same in the vernacular. Did he believe then? Did being on the altar mean anything more than being a patrol boy or playing on the baseball team? Was there a time when he did things that mattered to him, when he wasn't just going along?

It seemed to Kevin, that was the way he had come to live his life. He wrote, he studied, he occasionally drank, got high and had sex, in no particular order or combination. He wasn't committed heart and soul to anything except possibly photography. He could remember the first time he saw a picture come up in the darkroom. He would always remember it. It was magic. He set what looked like a blank sheet of paper in the solution and watched as the image appeared. Ironically, it had been a picture of Nancy. They were just friends then. He had found her on campus to show her the picture. He had actually run to her when he spotted her on the way to the Dining Hall. Kevin O'Connor didn't run, he sauntered. Kevin O'Connor didn't run and he didn't pray and he didn't get mixed up in complicated situations. At least he didn't until the cold, dark night that changed his life.

Now his soul had found its voice again. He prayed. He prayed with all the feeling he could summon, all the belief that he had ever known, everything in his life and soul that mattered. He prayed for Nancy and for Molly and for himself. He prayed for strength and for courage and for wisdom. Most ardently he prayed for grace,

CHAPTER VIII

As Molly began to unravel the Louise Porter murder, Nancy's attraction to the case became clearer. The photographs in the paper and in the yearbooks revealed a remarkably pretty girl. Yet, over the years, the only thing that people seemed to recall about Louise was the fact that she had married a seminarian. Long after the memory of the girl had faded, the hint of scandal remained. "The evil that men do live after them...." Shakespeare knew his craft. He knew people. Evil, real or imagined, leaves an indelible stain.

Louise Miranda, as she had been christened, had come to St. Anthony University from New York City. Not much was known about her family. She came from the big city to a small college town and never returned, not even in death. She was a member of the first few classes of young women who entered the University. St. Anthony had been, like many colleges and universities, a men's college. The 1950's was a period of change, some might say upheaval in America. It was Rock 'n Roll, Elvis Presley and bobby soxers, Dwight Eisenhower and the Red Scare. Millions of Baby Boomers were pouring out of high schools in search of a future that included post secondary degrees. Colleges, big and small, were feverishly constructing housing and adding classrooms to meet that ever increasing need St. Anthony was one of the first of a wave of men's colleges to open their doors to what some at the time still referred to as, "the fairer sex.."

Unlike most of her fellow co-eds, she had not found a warm welcome at St. Anthony. She had been awarded a scholarship, which might have been why she stuck it out. In her junior year she met Bob Porter and Tom Madden. The two men were roommates at the seminary adjacent to the University. Apparently, she acquired an association with the seminarians. Maybe she managed to find love.

During her college career, she sought affection from several other young men at St. Anthony. Obviously no one warned her how dangerous that could be. Kiss and tell is a favorite campus pastime and St. Anthony University proved no exception. .As Louise's search for warmth widened, her reputation suffered. Some people are popular and some people are not. The majority of any society lies somewhere in between. Most don't count their friends in double or triple digits, but they have friends to count. Louise didn.t.

Louise Miranda didn't. take her lack of popularity complacently. She didn't hide in her room or spend long, lonely hours studying in the library. Classmates remembered an independent, arrogant vixen, openly scornful of the rules and traditions of St. Anthony. Nevertheless, her hasty marriage to the young seminarian, Robert Porter still managed to send shock waves through the community and the subsequent slaying of the bride, less than three months following the wedding, added fuel to the fire.

Bob was never suspected in the murder. The day his wife was slain, he was working in a store in town. There were at least five witnesses who could attest to the fact that he had not even taken a lunch break that day. Many people thought that Bob Porter would return to the seminary following his wife's death. Instead, Bob gave up on God altogether. You couldn't blame him. From all accounts, Bob Porter was in love with Louise. He left the seminary just months before ordination to marry her. People figured he had made a bad bargain and were not afraid to tell him so. After the brutal killing of his wife, he just left. In the biblical sense, "shaking the dust from his sandals." .He died three years later trying to negotiate a hairpin turn at about sixty miles an hour. The end. There were rumors of suicide. Of course there were. Even in death, Bob Porter couldn't escape allegations, suppositions and turgid gossip.

Molly thought it wasn't the end. Someone had killed Louise Porter and had gotten away with it. Who had killed her and why? What had Louise done to warrant so brutal a death, so savage an enemy? What had Nancy uncovered to cause that killer to strike again?

Did the killer figure that what had worked once would work twice? Not this time, Molly answered. This time you pay. Kevin and she would methodically review Nancy's materials. They would dig deeper. They would work harder. They would solve the mystery. Kevin devised a system.

He scoured the yearbook files for the years that Louise attended St. Anthony. He uncovered the negatives of group shots, made contact sheets, did blow-ups, searching diligently for familiar faces and names. Nancy had said it was someone Molly knew. Therefore, it had to be someone on campus. That someone would have to have been on campus twenty years earlier and also would have to had some connection to Louise Porter.

Molly claimed she needed the alumni files for her senior thesis and received permission not only to access them on the school's computer, but to use the computer anytime day or night. She was told that Polly Kuyper in Housing would let her in the library or Jim Sutton from Security would provide her with a pass-key when needed. One thing about St. Anthony, they went out of their way to be accommodating. Their open-door policy was a little disconcerting considering that a student had just been murdered on campus.

Molly cross-referenced the alumni list with the list of present faculty and staff. Kevin went to the town library and ascertained copies of newspaper stories regarding the Porter murder. One problem surfaced immediately. Nancy had used the Kiernan influence to gain access to the actual case file. She had some notes on that, but the file itself was off limits to Molly and Kevin. Though neither admitted it, they were relieved. How could Nancy have looked at the gory pictures of Louise Porter?

They developed a list of suspects, but it read like a character list from a Russian novel. There were too many people without a viable motive in sight. Bob Porter was the only likely suspect and they knew he was innocent. Even if he had somehow managed to fool everyone and sneak off and kill his wife, .he couldn't have resurrected and killed Nancy.

The worst setback was Nancy's files. The murderer might as well have taken them for all the good they were to the investigation. The files were woefully incomplete, marked with reference letters and numbers, that neither Molly nor Kevin could decipher. Most importantly, Molly was acutely aware that she was running out of time. Registration for Spring Semester began in six days. Polly Kuyper had already called to see if Molly intended to return to the dorm.

"I hate to ask you so delicate a question, dear, but if you don't intend to live on campus this semester, we could certainly use your room. We would be glad to make the necessary adjustment in your tuition bill, but you'll have to let us know soon. '

Molly explained that she needed the room and that no adjustment would be necessary. She was embarrassed trying to explain her sleeping arrangements to Pollyana. (Miss Kuyper's unofficial title.) She had been caught off-guard. She hoped that Kuyper hadn't called Mrs.Monaghan. There was a moment's panic. Then Molly realized that there was an unwritten policy about privacy at St. Anthony. Many students spent week-ends or even weeks off campus.

"You never know with relationships," Molly said rather awkwardly, "I feel that I should have my own place, just in case." Molly would never give up her dorm room. It was true that some students moved off campus, but never the second semester of their senior year.

"A wise decision, dear." Polly cackled. Molly wondered if Polly had ever moved into a man's apartment. Naw, Molly concluded, "Nobody can get that drunk!" The minute she thought it, Molly was ashamed. It was a common phrase heard in the dorm. It was meant to be funny, just like, "He's too stupid to live." It wasn't witty or humorous, it was derisive.

Molly had uttered the phrase once at home. Her brothers had thought it hilarious. Her mother had not. "I don't like that." she stated. "It's unbecoming for you to say it." he added, "It's snotty. I never want to hear it again." Molly agreed with her mother, but sometimes she just slipped.

The call from Polly was a reminder that time was limited. Wading through old papers and books and trying to uncover a story mired in two decades of gossip and fading memories, Molly's nightmare had become reality. There was so much, out of which came too little. Not only were several faculty members St. Anthony grads, but half of the maintenance and security staff had also attended the college.

"My God, no wonder they say that St. Anthony has great job placement. They simply hire all their own graduates. It lends credence to the popular theory that inbreeding causes idiots." Kevin complained.

If Molly could just figure out Nancy's notes, she was sure that would make the pieces fit. Every day it seemed increasingly hopeless. The notes obviously referred to interviews, but where were the interviews themselves? Where was the list of people she actually had interviewed? What Molly had were preliminary notes, clippings of old newspaper articles, slips of papers with names and dates. They would have been enough for most students to write the story, but not Nancy. The in-depth stuff was missing. The knock-out questions and the all important answers, where were they? That's what Molly had forgotten to get from the room the day Nancy was killed. The most vital information, the answers that she and Kevin so desperately sought, that's what Molly had overlooked.

When Spring semester started, it would be over. One way or the other, it had to be finished. There were other considerations. She would have to move back to the dorm. She accepted that. Leaving Kevin would be like most things in life, a mixed blessing. She had become used to living with him. She was used to his presence. She marveled at his appetite for work, the speed at which he plowed through written material, his wit and his knowledge of things from African villages to car's innerds. He had an amazing facility with data and an inexplicable strange addiction to cartoons. She failed to comprehend how he could devour tacos at three in the morning, sleep restfully and awake clear-eyed and refreshed four hours later.

She liked the way that the apartment was an extension of Kevin's personality. It possessed that same order amid chaos that she had come to identify with him. She hated that he never remembered to put the toilet seat back down. She hated his sweat socks and sweat pants and sweat. She hated that he slurped all liquids. But most of all she hated the idea that he was probably more anxious for her to leave than she was to go. She would miss him. She knew that. When she went back to her room, surrounded by her familiar things and also surrounded by an entire building filled to capacity with other women, she would sorely miss Kevin O'Connor.

He, on the other hand, he with his traitor's heart, would probably be relieved Molly was back where she belonged. That hurt. That was the burr beneath the saddle. Kevin would be at home again, alone in his own place. At last, he would be free from Molly and her dangerous enterprises, free to bring someone else back to his apartment, someone who would not be relegated to the couch. He would, too. He was anxiously counting down the days. At least he had been polite enough not to carry on while Molly was there, but she knew that Kevin possessed no great appreciation for the positive aspects of celibacy. The strain was beginning to show.

My God, it's not like he was Mister Super Stud. According to Nancy and she was the best authority Molly could cite, Kevin behaved entirely too well, entirely too often. However, Kevin did seem to be showing a little stress under his and Molly's present living arrangement.

It might not be the lack of sexual activity at all. It could just be the frustration of trying to puzzle all of this out or perhaps, it was simply the combination. Kevin was used to living alone. When he did share his residence with a woman, it was usually over night or for a weekend and then there were certain activities bound to take the edge off things. Now, he was sharing his quarters with Molly, chasing a killer and living in what he considered both an unnatural and unproductive state. Even Molly felt the pressure.

Somehow she had finally located Limbo. She wanted Kevin and she didn't want him. That is to say, she was perfectly undecided. One moment she wanted Kevin to drag her into the bedroom and end all her indecision and the next she was grateful for the sibling atmosphere which surrounded their relationship. It was typical Molly! Once a day she would counsel herself "No regrets, no memories." She would risk it. After all, she was the right age to become involved in a sexual relationship. (Old, in fact, by most present standards.) But then she would list the negatives. The complex relationship she shared with Kevin might be permanently damaged by one roll in the hay. There was, also though she hated to admit it, the distinct possibility that Kevin might not want her. It was sexist to think that a man didn't care with whom he took his pleasure. What if Kevin felt pressured into going to bed with Molly? Wouldn't he bitterly resent her? It was too complicated, too demanding emotionally. Soon, Molly could go back to the dorm and things could return to normal. No more analyzing, no more philosophizing, no more tense moments that resulted from living together.

Kevin and Molly only needed to do one thing together - to find Nancy's killer and so far they were batting zero.

CHAPTER IX

Molly declared a day off. She piled anything vaguely connected either with Nancy or Louise Porter into the bedroom closet. It was time to open the windows and let in some sun. She reasoned if you look too closely at a picture you can easily miss what it represents. She wanted too much, she was working too hard. She was forcing pieces of the puzzle that simply did not fit. Enough. A day off would provide breathing space. Kevin took the day to catch up on some work in the camera shop. Since Kevin was busy downstairs until around five p.m., Molly decided to spend the day catching up on the soaps and chowing down on ice cream and oreo cookies, a worthy pursuit for a seeker of wisdom. Halfway through *All My Children* there was a knock on the apartment door. "Who is it?" Molly asked cautiously.

" It's Father Madden." Twice. This made twice that Molly had been surprised by the appearance of Father Tom.

"Okay, I'll be right there." Molly scanned the apartment for any tell-tale signs of the separate but equal life she and Kevin were living. She wondered if Father Tom was breaking yet another of his time honored rules by visiting off-campus apartments. Molly greeted him with, "Kevin's not here."

I came to see you. ."

Molly pointed to the bowl of ice cream. "Can I offer you anything - tea, coffee - a sundae?"

"I'll pass.

"How about a drink?" Molly suggested.

"I wouldn't want to deplete Kevin's supply of whiskey." he said snidely. A little sarcasm goes a long way. Still, she was rather fond of sarcasm, particularly Father Tom's. It made her feel at home.

"How about some of my scotch, then?" she asked. Molly was glad to see him, relieved in a way. She always felt stronger and safer in his presence and she especially needed to experience those feelings now. Molly was not about to allow one off the cuff remark to escalate into an argument.

"With a little soda, if you have it?" he asked tentatively.

"I do." Molly replied smiling. Father Tom followed Molly into the kitchen unabashedly opening drawers and peering into cupboards. Molly had never seen a housing inspector, but she was certain that he could take up that profession without additional training. "You seem to be fairly well stocked." he said in a surprised tone.

"Well, we're not prepared for a nuclear holocaust or the plagues of Egypt, but barring those eventualities, I think we'll make it." Molly was aware that she could never be accused of being Hannah Homemaker, but she wasn't poor Mrs. Hubbard" either. "What did you expect?" she asked. It was an earnest question, though it was tinged with irritation.

"I frankly didn't know what to expect. I just assumed that between paying for your dorm room and contributing to the rent here, you might be hurting financially. Molly, you're drowning the Scotch." he admonished. Molly tossed the drink. She handed the glass to Father Tom and commented, "You'd better make the drink, you're obviously better at it and for your information, I don't pay rent here."

"I see." The classic two word declarative/accusatory sentence. She hated the tone of his voice, the implication of the sentence. It worked on her like the sound of fingernails against a blackboard.

"Oh good. I'm so relieved. 'The blind shall see and the lame shall walk' Is that why you showed up here today - to find out, to question, to see, to judge?. God, don't look shocked, I would think with all the confessions you've heard, it would take more than a couple of college students living together to shake you up."

"I'm not shocked by the situation," he said defensively. "I'm disappointed in you." He was disappointed! Nice touch. He even looked the part, a walking sigh. Who could blame him? - Molly living in sin. Terrible. Heart-breaking. Disappointing. What did he expect of her anyway? She wasn't in the running for beatification. She had no intention of dying as St. Molly, virgin and martyr. He wasn't exactly 99.9% pure. She was fairly certain of that. That collar must be cutting off his circulation. ".Father" she started. She could hear the edge in her voice. She could feel her temper building but she had to catch herself. She couldn't let a moment's anger destroy whatever she and Kevin had achieved. If Father Tom was here it meant that the rumor had circulated and people were falling for it. She needed to play out the hand. He deserved to be told off, anyway--coming to visit her, bringing guilt as his housewarming gift.

"It's amazing, really," she continued. "Normally it takes forever to get in touch with you. You have classes and lectures and seminars to attend and sacraments to confer, there doesn't seem to be enough hours in the day for you to meet all your commitments to God and man. My God, I've been trying to corner you for an appointment for confession, since the beginning of December ... " He interrupted. "Normally, Molly, you are not in dire need of confession."

"Ah, I get it, the usual, boring species of everyday sin doesn't rate - say two Hail Marys and call me in the morning, but suddenly you figure I've departed my amateur standing, so I merit a house call. Good system. What do you call this - Sacramental Critical Care?'" Part of her was pleased that Tom would be that concerned. Part of her was insulted by the idea that just because she kept most of the commandments, her confessions were rated as not all that exciting, perhaps even a waste of time.

"Don't try and convince me that the reason you're living with Kevin O'Connor is because I've failed in my priestly duty toward you, it just won't wash." he announced.

What unmitigated gall. What incredible vanity. Molly was stunned. "Do you actually think that I would sleep with someone in order to attract your attention.--that I would live with someone, just to make you feel bad? That's sick. That is truly perverse. Really, Father, it's therapy time."

"It happens, Molly." he confided. He was all business. It was as if he were lecturing on the Nicene Council. "You wouldn't be the first girl to have a crush on a priest. We've been very close. It's not sick. It happens all the time and there is nothing very strange about it. It's normal. It just has to be handled properly." Molly was furious. It was one thing to be disappointed that she had succumbed to temptation. After all, he had taken a vow of celibacy. She knew that as far as her parents and Mr. Reardon and most priests were concerned, pre-marital sex was still a mortal sin. If Father Tom thought that Molly was imperiling her immortal soul, if he was concerned and maybe disappointed she hadn't battled natural urges to stay pure and ensure her spot in heaven that was one thing. To think that her sex life had anything to do with him, however was not only egocentric and self-centered, it was weird. *"It happens? It's normal..."* There was nothing normal about it.

Molly wanted to tear him limb from limb. Molly did not have crushes on teachers, on priests on coaches. They were people. She liked them or she didn't like them. She respected them or she didn't. It was simple, straightforward and squeaky clean. She didn't like it when professors married students or doctors became romantically entangled with their patients or administrative aides turned into administrative laids. It wasn't that any of those things were necessarily reprehensible, it was simply that they were part of that spongy area of morality that Molly desperately wanted to avoid. She cared for Father Tom but as a friend. She loved him, but within that context, within the boundaries she believed needed to exist. She had never to her knowledge, acted in a way which crossed those boundaries. But maybe she had. Maybe, when she thought she was speaking to Tom Madden in the manner of a young woman and a friend, he heard a girl in search of a father figure or a fantasy romance. It hurt her to think of her friendship with Tom in that light. It was time to pick up the pieces of her pride and set him straight.

"Father Thomas Owen Madden, listen very carefully. I don't care how many young girls have pined over you or how many hearts you've broken. I'm not the least bit in love with you. In fact, at this precise moment, I'm not even sure I like you very much. So don't worry about handling me properly or improperly. No handling is required! You can feel free to drink your drink in peace. You have my word that you shall not be molested. You are not my type"

"And Kevin is, I suppose?." he asked glumly. Now he was hurt. He had been all set for a replay of the Prodigal's Return --to welcome her back into the fold. He had expected her to pack up her things and allow him to play the forgiving Father. She had ruined his day.

"Kevin is a nice guy." she said, almost apologetically.

"He must be, more than nice, if you're so crazy about him that you had to move in here with him. Molly, can't you really live without him?" He acted as if he were asking her to give up a puppy. (Mom, he followed me home, can't I keep him?)

"I guess not." she said quietly. It was hard to lie. She had lied to her mother, to Mr. Reardon, to Polly Kuyper and now to Father Tom, her mentor, confessor and friend. Why had she answered the door?

"You *guess*? Molly, you're not the type of person who lives with someone because you guess that's the thing to do. I guess…I don't know…maybe…these aren't the answers for you. You can't build a future on those words."

Molly wondered what words Louise Porter had used for her decisions. Had she risked everything on a maybe or was she body and soul in love with Bob Porter? Molly hoped it was the latter. The girl deserved that much. Everyone deserves at least that.

Father Madden was on a roll now. He had been stumped for a moment, but now he had everything figured out. Alright, if Molly hadn't moved in to get even with him, then there must be another reason. Sex could be part of it of course. It was natural that it should be, although how anyone could be attracted to Kevin O'Connor in that way, was beyond belief. NO, he had thought about it and the reason that Molly was involved with this O'Connor person was obvious. He decided to explain it to her.

"Molly," he said, assuming the mantle of wisdom, "both you and Kevin have been severely traumatized by Nancy Kiernan's death. Out of your mutual grief you certainly could have established a common bond. Maybe both of you want to be in love with someone so much, you want to be in love with each other so much, that you're pretending that you do love each other. Maybe what you're feeling is indeed love, but it's not the right kind of love for a young couple to share. It's rooted in heartache and it will just provide you both with more of the same." Molly stared at her melted ice cream. It had turned ugly, not unlike the day.

"You're wrong, Father." she said. Father Thomas Madden did not accept defeat graciously.

"How am I wrong? You mean to tell me that your only interest in Kevin is sexual? Is he that good in bed that you refuse to move back to campus, lest you miss even one good lay?" Molly was outraged.

"I won't answer that. What are you, the reporter for the local tabloid? What if he is good in bed, what if that *is* the reason I'm here with him? Why should you care? Isn't that some form of voyeurism, for Christ sake? I can't believe you would even ask me those kinds of questions. How is my sex life your business or anybody else's? *Who are you?* I don't even recognize you. You're not the priest I knew. You're not my mentor or my friend."

"Molly, I will always be your friend. I will always care about you, even if you don't want me to. It's you who have changed or at least seem to have changed. If you thought what you were doing was right, Molly, you wouldn't be the least reluctant to talk about it. I know you, Molly. You'd be shouting from the rooftops." Knowing Molly was a seemingly common occurrence. Clare Tracey knew Molly and Kevin knew Molly and Father Tom Madden knew Molly. Only Molly was unsure about who she was. Too bad Molly hadn't killed Nancy, then everything would be simple. A murderer that well-known would be a cinch to nail!

"Father, I don't know how to break this to you, but shouting from the rooftops about sexual matters, just isn't in my make-up. With whom I have sex and where I have sex and why I have sex is relative only to me and the person with whom I'm involved. It is a very private and personal matter." Molly couldn't help it, she was impressed with herself. She could envision herself before an inquisition or a senate subcommittee. Molly Monaghan, the soul of discretion. Miss Monaghan, are you now or have you ever been…?

"Did you want me to hear your confession?" Tom asked.

"Why? Do you think I really want to confide in you, but I'm afraid you'll blurt it all out to the press? I don't need the seal of confession to make me feel protected. Let's just drop it." Molly suggested.

"Would you feel more comfortable with another priest, say Father Benedict?" Molly laughed. "Confessing to Father Benedict…that's a thought. Isn't that like doing a penance to receive one?" "He's a good priest, Molly." Priests were always sticking up for one another, adhering to that famed "United we stand" philosophy.

"Good or not, I have a confessor, at least I thought I did. You've been forgiving me and advising me and being a friend for almost four years. Are you trying to tell me, that just when things are getting interesting, you want to give it up?"

"Well, you know the pay's not good and the hours are long." There it was, finally – the smile, the warmth, the humor that she had spotted that long ago September. All that hurt and irritation was smothered by it, the emotional hug that existed between them.

"Ah, but think of the rewards: A crown in heaven and good scotch here below."

He smiled. No wonder young girls fell in love with him. "Good scotch and good company." he murmured.

"I can promise you good food, too, if you'd stay for dinner." Molly hoped he would.

"Will Kevin be here?" he asked warily.

"He does live here. Subsequently he's entitled to dining privileges. What have you got against Kevin anyway? You say his name like it's poison."

"He's arrogant and rude. I saw him the other day and I tried to talk to him. He walked past me as if I was invisible. He's not worthy of you."

"Well, of course, he's not worthy of me." Molly said laughingly. "Wherefore art thou who is worthy of me? Really, Father, I bet Kevin was not even aware you were trying to get his attention. When he's concentrating on something, he's just in a world of his own. I wouldn't take it personally."

"Well, I dislike him and I hope he takes that personally, because that's how it's meant.

"Hey, I thought you had to love everyone. Isn't in your contract?

"Love, not like…even priests are allowed to practice some discernment."

"Okay, but you're wrong about him." It was useless to argue. Tom Madden and Kevin O'Connor were too much alike. They were natural enemies. Molly walked him to the door. As she helped him on with his coat, he turned to her and explained:

"Maybe I am wrong about Kevin, but I can't believe that I'm this wrong about you. In the last couple of years, I thought I'd gotten to know you pretty well. I've watched you change, I've witnessed tremendous growth in you. I've been proud of you, counted on you. You've always touched me in a very special way and now suddenly you're not the Molly Monaghan I know. The Head of Housing comes up to me on campus and informs me that you're living here with Kevin. I didn't even know you were close to Kevin. I thought he was Nancy's boyfriend. Molly, I don't mean to embarrass you or to make you feel uncomfortable. Honestly, I came here today because I care about you. Promise me that no matter what you decide to do over the next months, that you'll remember that." Molly nodded.. "I promise." She almost said "Scout's honor," but the words caught in her throat.

"Okay. Now I'll give you my blessing." Molly bowed her head as he made the sign of the Cross over her. He uttered the familiar words: "May the Lord bless and keep you. May He make His sun to shine upon you. May He turn His countenance toward you and give you peace. In the name of the Father and the Son and the Holy Spirit. Amen." Maybe it was faith or more likely it was superstition, but Molly was grateful…grateful for a blessing, fearful of a curse. This was a symptom of too much Druid blood in Molly undiluted by generations of Roman theology. Warmed by such pleasant thoughts, Molly drank the remainder of her ice cream and faded into sleep.

CHAPTER X

"Good to see you're so alert." It was Kevin's voice. He was standing in the doorway of the darkened living room.

"I must have dozed off." Molly said as she turned on the lamp..

"Did you eat anything today? Kevin asked.

"Nothing terribly nourishing, ice cream and cookies." Kevin glanced at the glass on the table.

"Ice cream, cookies and booze?"

"No booze for me I had a visitor." Molly announced.

"A gentleman caller? I think that's breaking the rules. We'll have to solve this case and get you out of here before you scandalize the neighbors."

"I don't think they'd be too scandalized by this afternoon's visitor unless he showed up regularly, which he won't."

"Intriguing. Who was this mystery guest?"

"Father Tom."

Kevin was astonished. "You let him in here, while you were alone?"

"I've known him for four years. How could I refuse to let him in? If I had done that he would have suspected something. Besides, he would have been terribly offended. I couldn't do that."

"I wonder if that was Louise Porter's last thought?"

"Cut it out, Kevin. Father Tom doesn't have any reason to harm me. I can't believe he would ever hurt anyone. It just doesn't make sense."

"It makes sense to me. In both murders, he knew the victims, had plenty of opportunity and probably sufficient motive. That makes him as good a suspect as anybody else.

"The police never even questioned Tom about the Porter murder. Nan made a special mention of that in her notes."

"Let's see and that would be the same police who never caught the murderer of Louise Porter. Maybe they should have questioned the good Father. Maybe that's why Nan made special mention of it. Maybe she had come to the conclusion that Father Thomas Madden killed Louise Porter. She said she suspected someone you knew. Nancy made a point to interview him. We know that for sure. Maybe that's why she's dead."

"She interviewed several people. Tom Madden was Bob Porter's best friend, it only stands to reason that Nancy would interview him. It's got to be somebody else."

"Because he's a priest, right?"

"No, not entirely." Molly did not relish the role of defender of the faith.

"Right, not entirely. Maybe not at all. I don't think your stalwart defense of Tom Madden has anything to do with Holy Mother Church.

"Meaning?"

"Meaning, I think you have the hots for this guy."

That's disgusting."

"I agree. I thought you were above that, I would never have figured Molly Monaghan for a little god squader, a clergical groupie. No wonder these guys go haywire--all these women hanging around them, wondering, admiring, lusting after them. Watching and waiting for a break in the poor guy's vow of celibacy. It would not surprise me in the least, if one of these guys picked up a knife and created a few more Faithful Departed."

"Brilliant. You think it would be perfectly understandable for a priest to murder two women, as a release for his sexual frustration. Say, the way somebody else might work out in a gym or take a cold shower?"

Kevin stormed into the kitchen. Molly listened to the slamming of cupboards, the crashing of pans. She gave him a few minutes to cool off before she started to talk to him "Let's send out for a pizza, she suggested as she walked into the kitchen.

"I'm not done."

"Okay, but I thought we could order now and then maybe by the time it was delivered you would be done." She smiled. It seemed like a good idea.

"This isn't working." he muttered.

"All of this or part of this?" She was buying time. She had anticipated this. She had played out this discussion in her own mind, inventing Kevin's part in the dialogue. She wasn't sure how it would end. She was afraid she would have to pack up and leave. She knew she should stay, should be committed, but going home really sounded good. She wanted to go home, not to campus, but to her own bed and her own family, to safety and shelter and love.

"All of this, this living slash not-living together." Kevin answered. "It's driving both of us over the edge. Then there's the theory that if we keep up the pretense we'll convince the killer that he has nothing to fear from us, which should be easy since A. he doesn't and B. we haven't the slightest idea who it is we're trying to convince."

"Do you want double cheese, half-onions?" Molly was already dialing the phone.

"Are you listening to me?"

"Yes, I'm listening. I agree with you, but I don't know what to do.

"So, when in doubt order pizza?

"It's a good rule."

"Maybe that's the problem, Moll. You have rules for every occasion, but not everyone plays according to the rules, not your rules or those of society. You live in some sort of fantasy world where the bad guys get caught and the good guys always win. Life isn't like that. You've got to face reality. Admit it. We're not any closer to finding Nancy's killer, today, than we were the day after she was killed."

Molly had always taken her realism in large doses. She understood people didn't always play by the rules, but she believed in the rules anyway. She figured realism shouldn't necessarily negate decency. "I admit we don't exactly know who it is."

"We're not even close. We're not even in the ball-park." Kevin stated.

"I think we are." Maybe it was just fantasy on her part, but she believed it. She could feel it.

"You're just being stubborn." He wanted to add stupid, but thought better of it.

"You're being defeatist.

"Okay, I'll play. How close do you think we are? Will we know who it is tomorrow or the next day or next week or ever? Kevin demanded.

"Soon. We're close Kevin. I can feel it. We just have to keep going. It's like a math problem when you realize that you've been using the wrong method and that's why it's been so hard to come up with the answer. We've been using the wrong method. We only have to change strategy. We're just missing a couple of the pieces of the puzzle and then everything will fall into place."

"I love your analogies. They're so bad, they're beautiful. Puzzle pieces? Like who did it and why?!" Kevin was pacing back and forth like a caged lion. Molly had this terrible feeling that Kevin wanted to deck her.

"We know why Nancy was killed and we can assume that whoever killed her was the same person who killed Louise Porter. So we don't have to solve two murders. We only have to solve one. We have to be close to doing that.. Nancy did it with a hell of a lot less information than we've gathered. If she could figure it out, why can't we? We have her notes."

"This is where I came in. Molly, Nancy's notes are worthless. They're a mess. They might as well be hieroglyphics." He was weary of this. He wanted his life back again. He was tired of all the emotional and psychological strain, tired of Molly. She was too complicated and entirely too pig-headed.

"No. They're the key. The notes are just incomplete and I think I know why. It came to me today. I knew if I took some time off, it would help. I knew I was missing something the night I took Nancy's notes, but I just couldn't remember. Since then, I've been so busy concentrating on what information we can glean from the notes and complaining about how frustrating they were, that I just forgot. You know how it didn't make any sense that somebody as fastidious, as accurate as Nancy always was, could work from that mess?

Kevin nodded. They were both surprised by the incompleteness of Nancy's research,

"We knew all along that the numbers and letters had to mean something. Well, I think I've got it. Nancy had tapes."

"What do you mean she had tapes?" he asked incredulously.

"Nancy used to carry around one of those tiny, portable recorders in her purse. She taped every interview she ever had."

"That's illegal." Kevin was still in shock. Nancy had never mentioned anything about tapes to him. There was so much he didn't know, so much he had never bothered to find out.

"Yes, it's illegal and I think it's unethical, but Nancy did it."

"Are you sure?" Kevin always thought of Nancy as very legalistic. In fact, he imagined her more as a highly successful corporate lawyer than a writer. Molly was the writer, the girl who would struggle in some garret. She'd be more worried about whether a certain word sounded just right or not, rather than whether or not she had her rent money.

"I'm positive. Nancy and I had a huge disagreement over it. I lectured her about people having a legal and a moral right to know they were being taped. She claimed that she only used the tapes as reference. She said it was the only way of assuring absolute accuracy in an interview. She said that if she informed people that they were being taped, they objected or froze up and you couldn't get anything really significant from them. Whenever she interviewed anyone, she ran the recorder in her purse and that way she had an indisputable record of the interview verbatim. She didn't care about the ethics. It worked."

"Molly, I don't know whether to kiss you or kill you. How could you have forgotten this? It explains everything, but it doesn't really get us any closer to the truth. Where are the tapes? Wouldn't whoever ransacked Nancy's room have taken them and destroyed them?"

"It's possible, but I doubt it. Look how careful Nancy had been about all this. Suppose the killer had gotten hold of Nancy's notes, what would they have? Nothing without the tapes. I can't believe that Nan would have just left the tapes out in the open and even if she had, she wouldn't have labeled them, "interview tapes", not somebody who hides her written notes in her laundry hamper. Anyway, I'm pretty sure I'm the only one who knows they exist. No one else knew that Nancy taped people. Think of it, even you didn't suspect. No, those tapes are hidden and my bet is that no one has found them, not yet, anyway."

"So, do you think we could find them if you went through Nancy's stuff?" Kevin asked.

"Yes." Molly knew they could. Nancy would lead her to the tapes. Molly would use her heart and her memory as a divining rod. She would go to the well. She was close.

"They packed up everything from Nancy's room to ship to her family. It's all boxed up and stored in the yearbook office. They're going to pay for the shipping home. You have a key for the office. Right?" Molly asked tenuously.

Kevin was Editor of the yearbook. Molly knew he had the key. What she really needed to know was if Kevin was willing to let her search through Nancy's things or was Kevin finished with all of it? She could get into the office using some other pretext. Talking her way into someplace or around some rule had never been difficult for Molly She needed Kevin to still be in this. If he walked away now, she would be truly alone.

"We can go through the stuff tomorrow if you want." he said thoughtfully. Okay, Kevin thought. What could it hurt? Maybe she'll find them. Maybe she'll solve it. One way or the other, I'm closing this chapter of my life.

"Molly, even if the tapes are there," he warned. "They won't be easy to find. You said yourself that Nancy hid everything and who knows how careful they were when they packed those boxes? I don't think any of the cartons are labeled."

"I can find them and finally we can end this." Molly meant it.

"We're going to end this whether we find the tapes or not. Let's face it, we are not Sherlock Holmes or Jacques Cousteau .. "

"Hercule Poirot!"

Hercule Poirot? Are you sure?" Kevin grimaced.

"Yes. Poirot is Agatha Chritie's Belgian detective, Jacques Cousteau is the water guy. You know his ship, Calypso and all that."

"Calypso? Whatever. Tapes or no tapes, we're out of time. Next week, when the dorms open, we stop playing detectives. It's over.

CHAPTER XI

In the morning, Molly awoke to the smell of bacon and fresh coffee. She near-stumbled into the kitchen to find Kevin standing at the frying pan. "How do you want your eggs?" he asked nonchalantly.

"What's this?" she asked. In the time they spent together, mostly they had eaten take-out or delivery. Occasionally Molly had cooked. They never really had eaten a big breakfast. Kevin would usually have a bowl of cereal and rarely some toast. Molly might have toast or a doughnut, but generally was content with several cups of coffee and at Kevin's urging a glass of juice.

"Breakfast. I know you want to look for the tapes today, but I was thinking, let's just relax this morning. We can have a nice breakfast and do the crossword and talk about politics or school or anything or anyone except Nancy or Louise Porter. This afternoon I'll open the office for you and check on some yearbook business. How does that sound? e asked.

"God, Kevin, that's a great idea. Can I help?" She had had little sleep, worrying about finding the tapes, hoping that the killer hadn't found them first and destroyed them. Breakfast, eggs and bacon and juice and toast, followed by the crossword sounded wonderful. No wonder Nancy fell a little in love with Kevin. Whenever you thought you knew him, he did something totally unpredictable, something generous and thoughtful.

"How about making the toast? he suggested. Kevin looked happy. Molly realized a little guiltily that she had not paid much attention to Kevin. From the moment she learned about Nancy's death she had been focused on that and herself. She had relied on her family and Kevin and everyone else without giving any comfort or even acknowledging their considerable grief.

"Kevin," she said as she put the bread in the toaster. "I'm sorry."

Kevin cocked his head to the side. "About the toast?"

"No. I'm not sorry about the toast, at least not yet. I'm sorry to have been such a totally absorbed, emotional sponge. I'm sorry not to have asked even once how you're doing with all of this. I'm sorry that in trying to be the best friend to Nancy, I've been a really crappy friend to you."

Kevin smiled. "You've never been a crappy friend. You've been a pain in the ass sometimes but you're a great friend. If I wanted to talk about Nancy's death, I would. I'm just not built that way. You're giving me a way to do something about it, to channel my grief into an effort to find

Nancy's killer. Granted a visit to a shrink or a four day drunk would have provided safer therapy, but I'm still grateful. Today, though, this morning at least, I do need my friend to just be Molly. I want to have breakfast and just be us, the way we were before – just a couple of buds having a lazy morning. That's what I need. Can you do that?

"Absolutely. Yes, unequivocally, Yep, I'm in."

"And one more thing, it looks like you're having scrambled eggs…and really crunchy bacon. I'm thinking short-order chef may not be on the career horizon."

"How did you know? I love scrambled eggs and really crunchy bacon. It's what I order out." she said enthusiastically.

Kevin did most of the crossword puzzle. At about two in the afternoon, he drove Molly to campus. He unlocked the yearbook stockroom where they had stored Nancy's boxes. "Do you want me to help?" Molly shook her head. "I think it will go faster if I do it alone. "

"I'll be right in the office next door. Just knock on the wall if you change your mind or you need me."

A Sleeping Dog

The tapes were there and in typical Kiernan fashion. It took a little time, but the girls who had packed the boxes had been meticulous about labeling them. A sheet of paper taped to the top of each box named the contents. The packers had even sorted Nancy's clothes into "Winter casual" and "Winter dress, skirts and sweaters." Molly avoided the box labeled "Pictures."

Nancy had hidden the tapes among her music cassettes and records. They looked identical to several of the music tapes, the hand-written labels had artist's names and selections of songs listed on them. For extra insurance, Nancy had taped a song on the first part of each side of the tape. The clue was the number in the corner of each label. It corresponded with a number in Nancy's notes. Whoever broke into Nancy's room after her death had searched for Nancy's notes or any other material that might lead to discovery, but the murderer had ignored these. Nancy had won.

Molly gathered the tapes and placed them in an empty box. She stared at the other boxes and bundles in the room. Boxes, she thought. You die and they put you in a box and bury you. Then they box up the rest of what represents your life and it's over. She thought of all the times she'd moved. The Monaghans had lived in three different houses since Molly was born. Each time they moved things were at first, sorted carefully and packed tenderly with plenty of warnings on boxes containing fragile items. As moving day itself came closer, boxes began to contain more eclectic collections with only the name of the room where they should be unpacked. On moving day, cars were stuffed with furniture and photo albums, winter coats and various kitchen appliances. Molly compared the first time she came to St. Anthony and how little she returned to school with last September. This year when she left there would be fewer boxes than any other year. Most of what was worthwhile was in her heart and in her memory. Molly's thoughts echoed for a long time in a hollow space.

Finally, she thought, we are more than this. Dust to dust. There is more. She wasn't concerned about eternity or the hereafter. Here, there should be more here. There wasn't. There were memories and pictures and some stuff stuck in boxes that other people, even people that loved you, would file away and forget. Maybe Nancy knew that, maybe that's why she worked so hard. Maybe that's why she had investigated Louise Porter's death. Maybe she understood more about death, more about life, than Molly.

If you are a writer you can say something, you can type it in neat little letters and you can leave it behind you. It is not quite as forgettable as the dried corsage or the faded pictures or the other memorabilia of your life. Each time someone reads it, a little of you will come to them. A little of what you've experienced remains, a little of your life will rub off on them.

Instant immortality. Maybe it was worth it. Maybe? Maybe though, that little of your life that you left for the reader was lost to you forever.

Some cultures believe that when someone takes your picture he steals your soul. In a way that made sense to Molly. What happened when you mined your soul? Molly felt like she had lived her whole life like a character she was writing. When she looked in the mirror, she mentally described what she saw there as much as saw it. She looked at her changeable eyes, the eyes whose colors appeared in accordance with what she wore or the lighting in the room, sometimes brown or green or blue. On her driver's license they were listed as hazel. In the morning, in the mirror, while they were still sleepy, they were blue-grey.

She was both near-sighted and far-sighted, but Molly considered her eyes in-sighted. She had a habit of looking at someone or something so intensely that her eyes hurt. She was still listening, still caring, but she was also squirreling away what she heard and felt. She was memorizing the speaker's mannerisms, mentally filing away words and phrases. Molly studied her face each time she looked in the mirror, not vainly or critically, just for future reference. She would someday write a character and give her that face. In life, her face would change as she would change. Her skin would wrinkle and she would age but like Dorian Grey's portrait on some page, in neatly or perhaps not so neatly typed letters, that morning's face would remain forever unscathed.

She tried to do that now. She closed her eyes and tried to picture Nancy. She wanted to hear Nancy laugh. She wanted to look into Nancy's eyes and see the intelligence, the mischief, the humor - the life. It was too soon. The hurt got in the way. Words were just words. They were not life. They were ghosts of thoughts only.

Molly felt little and lost. She ran her hands over the boxes. Molly braced herself, but she didn't cry. She just remembered and let the memory hold her and then the memory turned into a prayer. She fell into some empty space, some sea of pain and darkness. She sat on the floor, her arms around the box of Nancy's tapes and chanted in a heart wrenching tone, "Help me, God, help me," as she rocked back and forth slowly. "O Sweet Jesus, help us."

Molly had to get away from St. Anthony. She and Kevin took the tapes to the apartment and spent the night listening to background information on the last few years of the life of Louise Porter. It was hard at first, to listen to Nan's voice, but there is a certain anonymity to the taped voice and they were listening more for what was being said than who was saying it. There were seemingly endless interviews with Porter's fellow students, teachers and the campus doctor. There were unfamiliar names and entirely too familiar names that cropped up again and again. There emerged a thumbnail profile of a girl, a woman who seemed destined to make all the wrong choices. She loved the wrong people at the wrong time and that cost her more than heartache. Somewhere along the line it cost her life.

People were not fond of Louise. She was beautiful and those less beautiful resented that. She was openly confused about life and those probably equally confused interpreted that confusion for arrogance. Men came to her aid. They wanted her. They loved her. They found her irresistible. Other women turned away from her. She was very much alone at St. Anthony. Around her sophomore year she starting spending time with Polly Kuyper. Polly seemed an unlikely associate for Louise.

Polly was quiet and shy. She had been born old. "an old soul". Even her student pictures in the yearbooks portrayed the eternal spinster, a prisoner of archaic phrases and sensible shoes. In some of the interviews, fellow students couldn't recall her name. One referred to her as "that mousey girl that was kind of weird." Polly had been the only child of an elderly couple who had worked on campus. Her parents were older when she was born. They were settled, somewhat simple people. She was raised at St. Anthony and would more than likely die there. What would have drawn her to Louise? Perhaps she had not been as intimidated by Louise as the other St.

Anthony co-eds. Neither of the girls would have seen the other as competition. Both having been ostracized, both outsiders. They may have forged a common bond. Molly was sure that Polly Kuyper could reveal a great deal about Louise Porter. There were other surprises among the list of Louise's intimates.

Apparently one of the men in Louise's life was a certain young and promising Journalism Professor. Doc was in his mid-thirties when he met Louise. There was never any real evidence that he and Louise had an affair. The rumors were pretty thick but then, there is never any shortage of those. Rumors are the life-blood of most communities. You take a young professor with a twinkling eye and a college student with a questionable reputation and if you don't come up with something juicy, you're the exception, not the rule. Louise apparently was involved with a series of men, including Doc, Bob Porter Tom Madden and Jim Sutton.

Jim was apparently head over heels in love with Louise. After his senior year, he stayed on at St. Anthony. He married a local girl and had a son who was presently a baseball star for the local high school. According to several of the people interviewed Sutton had taken Louise's hasty marriage and her subsequent death badly. He spent a few years trying to climb out of the wrong side of a bottle, but he had straightened out. He was in charge of Security on campus and had been for the last ten years.

A Sleeping Dog

Bob Porter was an enigma. He would have been suspect number one except that he was dead. Death ranks as an excellent alibi. From all reports, he had been the kind of guy that restored your faith in humanity. He was from upstate New York, but those who didn't know that figured he was from the mid-west. He had a country boy charm that was out of place at St. Anthony. When he was eighteen, he found that he loved God and his fellow man with a consuming fire. So he entered the priesthood because that was the thing to do. When a few years later, he discovered that Louise Miranda lit a different kind of fire for him, he left the priesthood and married her, because that was the thing to do. But when he was suddenly summoned home one day to identify what was left of his wife and to answer deeply personal and complex questions for people who seemed like they had never understood any kind of fire, there didn't seem to be anything to do.

Molly envied that kind of all or nothing love. In a weird way, she was jealous of the way he just did what he believed, what his heart wanted. Of all the characters in this seeming melodrama, she was sorriest for him, not because of the scandal or even for the slaying of his wife, but because "people talk." Those same fellow students and friends and teachers and neighbors who said what a nice guy Bob was, then maligned the person he loved more than life. Why? Molly thought it wasn't the killer who was responsible for Bob Porter's demise. It was gossip and innuendo. Molly wished he had survived that. She wished that somehow, like the other men in the Louise Porter story, he had found a way to go forward. Yet in a way it was fitting that he not. It was almost as if he was on borrowed time after they found Louise's body. He had given his heart and soul to the Church and then to Louise and he lost both. Perhaps he had nothing left. Molly thought the world was very much diminished by his loss.

Tom Madden and Bob Porter had been best friends. They were seminarians together. They were together when they met Louise. Several people interviewed were surprised that Louise became Mrs. Porter and not Mrs. Madden. Molly tried to imagine Tom Madden married but it didn't work. Yet it was hard to comprehend any of the pictures that the interviews were creating. It was hard to imagine any of the people in these interviews as murderers, twenty years ago or now.

"Kevin," Molly said suddenly. "I don't know. Do you think maybe we're wrong? Maybe the two deaths aren't connected. Maybe the murderer isn't any of the people mentioned in these tapes and we'll never get him."

"I agree with you that we might never figure out who it is, but I think it's for sure one of the people mentioned in these tapes. I just can't figure out which one." They compiled a new list of suspects. The requirements were motive and opportunity. Since it was hard to determine a twenty-year old motive, a suspect had to have been linked somehow with Louise Porter and in addition, he or she would have to also have had the opportunity to kill Nancy. Kevin took out a paper and began to write. First suspect?"

"Jim Sutton. Motive - jilted lover" Molly ventured.

"Do you really think people kill over *that* in real life?" he asked cynically.

"Don't you?"

"I doubt it. I think they just get a little drunk and start listening to a lot of country western songs."

"Interesting. I suppose you never heard of crimes of passion." Molly asked sarcastically.

"I've heard of them, but they always sound more like crimes of bad temper or homicidal rage or drunken or drugged up violence." Kevin explained.

"What about the baby?" Molly suggested.

"What baby?" Kevin was shocked. He wished Molly would stop pulling rabbits out of hats. ...."Nancy's interview with the campus doctor. He said that he told Louise she was pregnant the week before she was killed. What if Bob wasn't the father? Nancy used the pregnancy as a hook in her interview with all the prime candidates."

"How did I not get that/" Kevin wondered aloud. He had listened to all the tapes with Molly. He suspected, though, that he had missed a lot of what was on those tapes. It was torture to hear Nancy's voice. He couldn't admit that to Molly. He just thought of other things while the tapes played.

"Okay. Jim Sutton - suspect number one. Certainly nobody would have thought it weird for him to be in the parking lot when Nancy was killed. He's a possible."

"Who else?" Molly leaned back and thought. "You might not go along with this, but I think Polly Kuyper could have done it."

"'Polly Kuyper?. St. Anthony's own Pollyanna? Be real! The only people she's dangerous to are diabetics!" Kevin said snidely.

"Hear me out on this. Polly was really the only woman close to Louise. Suppose she was jealous of Louise? That jealousy could erupt. What if she had fallen in love with Bob Porter or Tom Madden or any of the guys connected with Louise?"

"Or maybe Louise." Kevin interjected.

"Okay, maybe Louise." Molly was willing to consider any possibility, though it was hard enough to imagine Miss. Kuyper as heterosexual, let alone Lesbian. Molly continued with her theory, "In her interview with Nancy, Polly admitted that she had suffered a nervous breakdown after Louise's death. Suppose there was justifiable reason for that breakdown."

"Louise's death might have triggered that, especially if they were close. Look at what Nancy's death has done to us. If we didn't have each other…" He hesitated. "I think you're reaching on this, Molly. I'm all for women's liberation and equal rights and the rest of it, but I don't know if I can buy it. Maybe a woman could have killed Louise and Nancy, but why not Mrs. Pascari or Mrs. Sutton or another co-ed? If jealousy's a credible motive, I'm going to need more paper."

"Mrs. Pascari was in Europe when Louise was killed which is probably why there was a rumor about Louise and Doc to begin with and Mrs. Sutton wasn't in the picture yet.

"Still, I don't know. The murder of Louise was pretty brutal. You think that a friend, even a disturbed friend could do that to somebody? Besides. she's. kind of timid, isn't she? You know her better than I do, but I don't see it.

"Quiet types can be dangerous. Nobody even notices them until they blow." Molly couldn't help feeling she was echoing Clare's theory of explosive emotions.

"All right. All right. Suspect two - Polly Kuyper. Now let's get to the ones you're trying to avoid."

"Such as?

"Such as your friendly friar, Tom, for example."

"The motive being that he was in love with Louise?" Molly didn't believe it.

"Maybe he was in love with Bob Porter?" Kevin suggested.

"What's up with you? First, Polly Kuyper and now Tom? I think that's sick. You sound like some weirdo murmuring about the strange goings on in monastery basements."

"Okay, forget the limp wrist comment, even if he is totally heterosexual, he's still a prime suspect. You commented on his interview twice, yourself. You said that he had been very cool, almost formal until Nancy brought up his involvement with Louise. Then he lost it. He practically tried to excommunicate her. He's hiding something and he's my bet for top of the list."

"I know." Molly conceded. Nancy unnerved Tom Madden and it didn't make sense. There was something there, however hard it was for Molly to admit it. She couldn't help but remember that Tom had been looking for Nancy the night she died and that he had told Molly to tell Nancy to stop what she was doing. Molly had not shared that information with Kevin. She was afraid it might be misconstrued. It bothered Molly. What if there were more to Tom's visit to Nancy's dorm room? What if he had visited Molly, at Kevin's, for some other reason than concern for her heart and soul? Tom Madden was acting very out of character and it was troubling, maybe even suspicious.

"It's possible and we're discussing possibilities. Suspect number three - Father Tom Madden. Anybody else?

"What about that mumbo, jumbo guy, Brother Whosis? He wasn't even at the funeral."

"That's because he's on retreat in Austria or someplace. He left Thanksgiving weekend and won't be back until May. That's why I didn't even check to see if he was here when Louise Porter was a student. I don't think he was. I'm pretty sure that he first came to St. Anthony last year. Anyway, he wouldn't have known that Nancy was on the story. So, he's out. Other ideas?"

"Your other friend. Doc. You know, Moll, when this is all over you might be more

discriminating about your role models." Kevin said sarcastically..

"Cute. Okay, Doc's included. I figured he would have to be. His interview with Nancy was strange. In all the other interviews she just about hammers people to the wall. Yet, with him, she only hints at what she's really after. She tiptoes around the issue. It wasn't Kiernan style. Maybe she just couldn't think of Doc as a suspect"

"Maybe that's what got her killed."

"You know, another thing is kind of weird. The day Nancy was killed we talked about Doc. It was almost ominous now that I think back on it. I asked her if she ever thought he had had an affair. She jumped all over me about it. Yet she was sitting on all this. It doesn't make sense. She had been privy to all this innuendo and rumor." "

"Then it fits. Anything that doesn't make sense belongs with this case." They sat there for a while looking at the list and thinking. They were waiting for a plan to develop, hoping that an idea would appear and they could set things in motion. All the time secretly praying no plan would take root.

The names on the list represented people, good people, people who had touched their lives in extraordinary ways. Neither Kevin nor Molly genuinely wanted to prove that any person on that list was a murderer. Even if they had wanted to, they weren't sure how they could.

"What now?" Kevin asked finally.

"Now we let him think I've got him" Molly answered.

"What?"

"Now I go to each of the suspects and tell each one a little about all of this. I'll say that I've discovered the tapes and that I'm planning on turning them over to the police."

"So?" He was listening. That's what had gotten him into all this in the beginning. He had to stop listening to Molly.

"So somebody is already very nervous, nervous enough to go through Nancy's room to look for possible evidence, precisely the kind of evidence that could be on these tapes."

"So then this person will be after you?" He couldn't be getting this right. It sounded like she wanted the murderer to try to kill her.

"Yes," It's the only way we can get the killer to show his hand."

"It's not smart." Kevin insisted.

"There's no alternative. It's the only plan I have. I'm not crazy about it myself, but what are the choices?"

"It's not smart!" He said again, shaking his head. like a toddler refusing to eat his strained carrots.

"Stop saying that. I know it's not the Rhodes Scholar's plan to catch a murderer. But I think it will work."

"I know it won't."

"How do you know it won't?"

"Because I won't do it and I won't let you do it. I'll call the police. I'll tie you up and keep you here if I have to. You could probably use some bondage in your life anyway.

"You said you wanted this ended."

"Yes, I wanted *this* ended. Not you ended. I can't deal with another death." He worried about Molly. She had this Irish penchant for tragedy. When she'd go home over semester breaks she'd spend most of the vacation attending wakes and funerals and benefits. He once asked her if everyone migrated to her hometown to die?

"I'll be careful, Kevin and you can protect me."

"What if this confidence in me is unwarranted? You don't even know what I'm up against." It was senseless to argue with her. Molly would say something then walk away. She would tune out anything she didn't want to hear. Yes, she knew it was dangerous, but then wasn't this the same risk that had always been present. Yes, she knew it could backfire, but there had always been that possibility as well.

Yes, she knew she could be killed, but she was angry. She was afraid and she was infuriated by that fear. There were other feelings, feelings she could not share with Kevin. She was already thinking out of a hole deeper than six feet. She was haunted by a pile of boxes in a stockroom, by the eyes of Nancy Kiernan, by the ache of her own grief and the depth of her confusion.

Tomorrow didn't matter. She couldn't daydream now about a home and family, about a flock of little Mollies, about a book with her name under the title. Maybe she would get those things and maybe she wouldn't, but today she would say something. She would look at somebody, somebody who thought he (or she) had the right to eliminate others, somebody who figured that he could just take other people's lives. She would look straight through that person. She would stare into his warped little soul and he would know that she knew. Molly had to do it. She had to open up that bastard. She had to turn the terror around. No more games.

Kevin reluctantly agreed with the plan. He would act as backup. He would hang around Molly and try to save her from being murdered. Kevin did not feel pleased with the situation. After Molly went to bed, he took out her wallet and located a business card, with a long distance number. Kevin decided it was time to invest in a little insurance.

"Hello. Is this Jeremiah Reardon? Kevin asked.

"Speaking."

"I'm sorry to call you so late. You don't know me. I'm Kevin O'Connor, a friend of Molly Monaghan…

CHAPTER XII

Molly rose early and after three cups of coffee, she made appointments to meet with the heads of the following departments: Housing, Security and Journalism. She then called the Friary and asked Father Tom Madden to hear her confession later that evening. She went to the box of Nancy's tapes and took out the tape recorder. Molly checked the batteries and loaded a blank tape in the recorder. Then she slipped the recorder into her bag. This time she would do it Nancy's way.

. The Security Building at St. Anthony looked like a bomb-shelter with a glandular condition. It was a squat, concrete building which housed three or four offices. In more militaristic times it had been the home for the campus' ROTC office. Those were other times and when the ROTC sought greener pastures, the Security department inherited the building. St. Anthony Security Staff consisted primarily of upperclassmen who were involved in the Work Study Program. The office was open 24 hours and usually a visitor was met by a young man, feet up on the reception desk, finishing some required reading. Today was the exception. Jim Sutton met

Molly in the reception area and ushered her into his office. "Looks kind of empty around here," Molly said warily. Jim shrugged. "Semester break. I'm left minding the store."

Jim Sutton seemed out of place in an office. He was a big man. He was actually only about 6'2 inches in height, but he was built solidly. The word mammoth sprang to mind. When he took Molly's hand to shake it, she began to worry that Kevin may have been right about this plan. Yet, it didn't seem likely that Jim would stab somebody. He could shake the life out of them if murder was his intention. The problem all along was that nobody who might have done it seemed like a person who could have done it. Molly asked Jim about the missing cinder blocks from the construction site.

"Molly, I thought that paper was finished. I pretty much figured you solved the case of the missing blocks." He smiled.

Molly figured Jim knew where the blocks were located. He didn't seem to miss much. That was his way. It made you wonder if somebody so conscientious about little things, could let Nancy's murder just fade into the woodwork?

"I almost solved it, but then things got a little harried. When Nancy Kiernan got killed, I guess I put everything on hold."

"It was a terrible thing all right, but I'm glad you're getting back into the swing of things. When someone close to you dies, it can knock you for a loop. That doesn't mean you should stop living"

. Molly looked at the man opposite her, his broad chin and crewcut. She wondered if he had picked up this philosophy before or after Louise Porter's death. She wondered how many mornings after brought him to this conclusion.

"Yeh, I guess you're right. But Nancy's death hit me rather hard. We were close. She was my best friend." Molly could say that now. Nancy had been her best friend. "We could confide in one another, trust each other."

Jim nodded. He looked serious. Molly had seen him look like this more than once. It wasn't as if there was a lot of crime at St. Anthony, but there was the occasional brawl or an accident in the parking lot. He had a way of listening that expressed the gravity of the situation. If you were trying to get out of a parking ticket, for example, you knew he didn't really care. He would still listen, but with a certain bemused expression. In her four years, Molly never knew of a single ticket that was paid. The theory was that Sutton handed them out just to collect interesting and creative excuses.

"In fact, the day she died, Nancy gave me some tapes." Molly continued, trying not to let the fear creep into her voice. "Did you know that she was investigating the Louise Porter killing that occurred about twenty years ago? She taped some interviews during the course of the investigation."

"She interviewed me about that, but she didn't tape it." he said, matter-of-factly.

Molly smiled. "She probably did. She taped all her interviews. She carried a little portable recorder in her purse. Molly waited for a reaction, but Jim Sutton gave nothing away.

"Mr. Sutton, did you work the night Nan died?"

"Why?"

"I don't know, but I was thinking maybe you would have noticed somebody."

"What are you up to? I answered all these questions for the police. I'm not going to go through this with you. Is this for the paper or something?" Molly had worked for the last three years on the campus newspaper. She had many by-lines, including a couple Page 1 stories, *above the fold*. She hadn't thought about it, but it was perfectly logical, though a bit callous, for Molly to cover Nancy's murder.

"Yes. I guess since we were so close, the editor thought I'd want to write the story. I haven't really talked to the police, yet. I don't know what they asked."

"They asked me plenty. Just in case you weren't aware of this, murder is hardly the order of the day at St. Anthony. Why the sudden lack of confidence in the police?"

"Because they never caught Louise Porter's killer and they'll probably never catch Nancy's."

Jim stared at Molly. "You think it's the same person?"

"I do and I think Nancy knew who it was."

"You could be wrong. I didn't know Nancy very well, but I doubt that she solved a twenty year murder case. My memory from that time is a little foggy. In fact, I told Nancy that, but I remember the police worked very hard on that case. If they didn't find the murderer, it was probably because he didn't stick around. Nancy Kiernan's killer might not have even been born when Louise Porter died.

"You don't believe that."

"What are you talking about? Of course I believe it. Your theory is, I take it, that the same person killed both girls?" Molly nodded in affirmation.

"Let me get this straight. You think that there's this killer, who stabs Louise Porter in town twenty years ago. He doesn't get caught and he sticks around until Nancy Kiernan appears. Then he comes out of retirement to kill her on the way back to her dorm room on a college campus."

"Yes, pretty much."

"You don't think that Nancy could have been murdered by some maniac, who saw an opportunity and took it? Jim added. "Or that it could be in the realm of possibility that Miss Kiernan pissed off some other less than stable fellow student?"

"No, I think she found out who killed Louise Porter."

"Then why not take that theory to the police? Maybe they could use your help." There was more than a hint of sarcasm in his suggestion.

"I intend to, along with her tapes. Mr. Sutton, Nancy said you knew Louise Porter. I thought if you were working the night Nancy was killed, you might have noticed if somebody else who also knew Louise happened to show up. You know, a face you hadn't seen in a long time. You wouldn't have thought anything about it at the time, but now, if I'm right…" Molly had to rephrase it, but didn't know how.

"If you're right, what? Is this where I'm supposed to say, 'Oh yeah, come to think of it, I did run into so and so that day. Hadn't seen him since Louise Porter was killed. He kind of looked like he was carrying a knife, too. Be sensible, Molly, I'm Head of Security, not Sam Spade. Now if your car has been broken into or somebody stole your purse, then maybe I can help you. This is sheer craziness." .He could feel the pounding in his head. The nightmare continued. First Nancy Kiernan now the Monaghan kid. Didn't the teachers have any control over these kids? He had already complained to Pascari and the Dean. Why couldn't they keep their noses out of where they didn't belong.

"The killing of Louise was a life time ago. I told your friend Nancy that, when she came nosing around. What do you girls think you're playing at? If you're right, then you're putting yourself in tremendous danger. I don't know what you think I can do about any of this."

"You knew Louise. You were involved with her. You probably knew the killer. That's why Nancy interviewed you. There might be something that you remember

"To be honest, I don't remember much about that period. Look, Molly I'm an alcoholic. Louise Miranda didn't help things, but she wasn't responsible. Maybe I was in love with her, maybe not. She certainly wasn't good for me, but then to be honest, she wasn't much good for anyone. I was no day at the beach myself. I hit bottom after she died, but I got better. I've been sober since the birth of my son. I'm not who I was back then. I don't want to relive those days and there are a lot of people around here who feel the same way." He wondered if Molly believed him. She was kind of scary. She stared at him so intently. It wasn't like Nancy Kiernan. Kiernan was accusatory, tough as nails. Monaghan looked sad, empathetic. Tapes. Were there tapes? How damning were they?

He had said he didn't remember Louise. He remembered everything about Louise. He recalled every cruelty, every humiliation, every regret. He could say that what had happened hadn't been Louise's fault, but even when he said it, he could hear the protestations of his heart. Why didn't they understand? Things were better, healed. These kids didn't have a clue. They were opening Pandora's box. If Molly suspected Sutton how stupid was she to come alone to his office? He shook his head in dismay.

"Then your advice would be to take my theory and the tapes to the police?" Molly asked.

"My advice is and you should take it, Molly: Forget about the tapes and forget about the police. Let the dead bury the dead. Stick to missing bricks. Now if you don't mind, Miss Monaghan, Get out of here. I'm sure you can find your way out." He didn't walk Molly to the door. As she left Molly took one last look at Suspect Number One. He was busy rifling through his desk drawers. She wondered if he was searching for something connected to Louise Porter or whether he had just misplaced something more mundane.

His statement could be interpreted as a warning, but more than likely it was simply sound advice. Molly had tried to open Jim Sutton up. She couldn't tell if she had touched a nerve or not. Basically she had come up empty and she knew it. That was okay. At least, he had provided her with a more plausible reason for her interview with Doc. She hadn't expected any of the suspects to leap at her. She was just planting a seed. She was saying, 'Look what I've got' and asking 'How much do you want it? You'll have to get me to get it. That was the message she was conveying to people with whom she spoke today. Molly was just laying the bait. It was unfortunate that the bait was her life.

CHAPTER XIII

Doc offered her a cup of coffee when she came in the office. The office walls were dull institutional grey, but they were crowded with pictures of former Journalism students who had made good. They were success stories to ponder while you waited for Doc to critique your paper or charm you with some ancient anecdote.

"Miss Monaghan, tell me what this is all about." he asked smilingly. "I heard that you had returned to campus early and that you had begun work on your thesis. That certainly is good news. Is there some way I can help?"

"I have to talk to you about Nancy Kiernan." Molly answered earnestly. "I'm writing a piece for the paper about her murder."

"That's going to be tough for you, but it's a good editorial decision. No one could do it better." He let Molly bask in the compliment for a moment.

"Well, Nancy was a brilliant student, but of course, you know that. I had great hopes that Miss Kiernan would bring substantial honor to this institution." Not to mention substantial funding, Molly thought.

" Her death was a terrible waste. She was the shining light of your class. There was no doubt about that. There was something very special about that girl. My God, she could burn up a page." They were quiet then. Molly and Doctor Pascari. They sat for a few moments and listened to each other's anguish. Once Nancy had written this satiric piece on an Albany politician, that was unmerciful. It was funny and sophisticated and politically astute, but it barely left the guy breathing. Nancy had wit and intelligence in her writing, beyond that she had power. Her words were lethal. In her poetry, Nancy was gentler, but the power was still there. Molly thought about Doc's "Shining light." She thought about how that light was brutally extinguished in a nearby parking lot. That thought made Molly crazy. People do stupid things when they are crazy. "Doc, did you have an affair with Louise Porter?" Molly asked.

"What?" He was obviously both startled and outraged by the question.

"Nancy was investigating Louise Porter's death. That's why Nancy was killed. Whoever killed Louise also killed Nancy and I'm going to prove it." Staring at Doc, her voice steady and hard, she could feel her anger rising. This man, whom Nancy trusted, whom they all trusted, may have taken her life. At the very least, he was connected to it, this scholarly gentleman so grieved by Nancy's loss.

"I'm going to prove it. I've got tapes," Molly yelled. "Evidence. I'm going to give them to the police. I'm going to prove it."

"Molly, Molly, calm down. Listen to me. Tell me slowly, calmly what you're talking about." Molly felt totally defeated. Doc didn't kill Nancy and Jim Sutton didn't kill Nancy and Tom Madden didn't kill Nancy and Polly Kuyper didn't kill Nancy. Nobody killed Nancy, but Nancy was dead. Puppies chase their tails sometimes, they run around in circles till they drop and Molly was within inches of dropping. Outside the office, Kevin was getting very nervous. This wasn't smart and this wasn't working and he wondered if he should call his new found friend the detective and report in and resign once and for all from this business. I take pictures, he thought, that's what I was meant to do. What am I going to do if I do catch the murderer, ask him to smile so I can get a good shot!

Molly wanted to stop. She couldn't believe that she had yelled at the Chairman of the Journalism Department. None of this seemed very real anymore.

"I'm sorry Doc. I've been a little crazy since Nancy's death. Did you know that Nancy was investigating the death of Louise Porter for her assignment for your class?" Maybe Molly could explain this all, but she sincerely doubted it.

"I was aware of it. Nancy ruffled quite a few feathers around here. When feathers get ruffled by a Journalism student, I usually am made aware of it, but then that was part of Nancy's MO. She could be very biting, sometimes unnecessarily so. It was her style, Molly, not yours. You speak to people's hearts. You're gift is as great as Nancy's, maybe greater. I shouldn't need to say that to you, but I feel I must. I wish you had some of Nancy's ambition. There's no denying that, but Nancy could have used some of your feeling." He was not the old world gentleman now. There was none of the charming yet distant courtesy which marked most of his conversations. His tone was friendly, sincere, paternal. Pascari knew his students better than most professors. Maybe it was because who they were was revealed in their writing. He didn't have to have drinks with them in the skeller or attend their parties or socialize with them outside of class. He rarely attended a basketball game or a concert and yet he knew them better than their own families. It was in their words and phrases, the way they went after a piece, the story angles they chose. He saw it in class when they discussed authors and topics and writing. They were writers, all of them. Some wanted to write sports and some news and some features and almost all of them dreamt of seeing their own bylines.

He knew who among them sought fame and who sought truth and who were naïve enough to believe that you could do both at the same time. He suspected Molly might be one of the truth seekers. He hoped that she would survive despite that.

"That feeling won't let me walk away from this." Molly confided.

"I think it will. Is that why you came to me today, to ask me about Nancy's story?" The professional tenor was back in his voice..

"I came to ask you what Nancy didn't. Before Louise Porter became Louise Porter, she was a student of yours, a student who seemed to then warrant a great deal of your attention. Your wife was away at the time on Sabbatical or something. There were plenty of rumors surrounding your relationship with Louise."

"I was aware of the rumors." Pascari did not attempt to hide the irritation in his voice.

"Were they based on truth?"

"That's none of your business and you know that. The question is totally inappropriate and invasive at the very least." He was critiquing her interview.

"I have to ask you." Molly said apologetically.

"Why? Why would you ask me that? What kind of poison has seeped into your mind. A bright mind, Molly, a fine mind. What would make you believe twenty year old slander? With what authority do you suppose you have the right to pry into people's past?" he demanded.

"I don't believe it, but I need you to tell me about Louise. Why would somebody murder her?"

"All right, Miss Monaghan. You don't really need to know and you have no right to ask, but I'll tell you anyway. You want to play at gossip columnist. I'll go along. Louise was eminently murderable. She was remarkably pretty. Quite beautiful. Her face was like porcelain, with just the right amount of blush to her cheeks. She never wore make-up. She didn't color from a jar. Her eyes were light blue crystal, covered in the longest, blondest lashes I have ever seen. She was very attractive. Sometimes when the light caught her a certain way, she was so remarkable that your breath would stop. No photograph could ever truly capture it. Beyond that, she had a quality all her own, quite unique. A kind of mystique. She looked the epitome of innocence. She was not. In many ways she was the complete antithesis of how she appeared." Suddenly, Pascari stopped, as if he were picturing her again. He sighed, "so beautiful, so seemingly vulnerable. I remember the first time I criticized her work. She cried. Right in the middle of the classroom, she wept as if she had just witnessed the love of her life cut down in front of her. I was devastated. I think I would have died for her at that moment. She had that power. She could make a man feel sixteen, all acned and awkward. She used that. She played with me for awhile. Flirted with me quite openly. I encouraged her to do so. I wasn't in love with the girl. I was *amazed* by her. I had all my life been surrounded by books and writers, stories of fatal attractions which had escaped me totally and then I ran into Louise. I made a fool of myself and I didn't care. I risked everything, my marriage, my position, everything."

He remembered. He took her to dinner, for long drives, early morning coffees. His wife, his beautiful, smart, good wife was half a world away studying Renaissance artists. He was here being a fool. He was mesmerized. Sometimes she was attentive and sometimes she was petulant. She made him giddy. He came to campus everyday looking for her, disappointed when she failed to make an appearance. If she showed up outside his classroom, he'd dismiss early, so he could walk with her and talk with her. He should have been discreet. He wasn't. Part of him liked not caring. He was a writer, not just a teacher. His whole life he had played by the rules of society. He wasn't a drunk. He didn't take drugs. He'd never before even considered being unfaithful. *He was a writer and this was his one moment to be crazy and passionate and reckless.* Even when he was miserable, he had never felt more alive. It was like standing on the precipice of a mountain. It was invigorating and terrifying.

Still, after all these years, simply talking about it brought it back --the exhilaration and the humiliation. When she moved on, when he was used up and she was tired of him, he should have been relieved. He was angry and disappointed and looked to himself and he suspected looked to others, ridiculous. Louise didn't just leave him. She didn't just walk away. She taunted him. In retrospect, that had been the test he passed. In the end, he was still employed and Louise was dead. Students graduated, his wife returned and Pascari survived. He survived Louise but at no little cost.

Molly was staring at him, waiting for an explanation. He had none. Molly didn't understand cruelty. Nancy might have, but she hadn't asked and he wouldn't have told her anyway. Molly had no hard edges. Why did she have to delve into the cesspool? It hurt him to see the disappointment in her face. He liked Molly. She was bright and funny and irreverent. She made him laugh. She was funny and could find humor in the least likely places. Often that same humor showed up in her writing, some phrase or peripheral comment that would cause the reader to smile. Yet there was an underlying quality of strength, both in everything she wrote and in the girl herself. She had heart. How ironic that she should care about Louise Porter, who had a heart of stone, if she had one at all? Louise Porter...

"She didn't care about what it might cost me. I suppose that was why she bothered with me at all-- the possibility of scandal. She reveled in it. at least, for a while, but then it bored her. She moved on to Bob Porter. She did a number on Tom Madden and Bob Porter that I have never seen equaled." Pascari figured Molly already knew, at least, part of this. If she knew about his involvement, then she probably knew about or at least guessed Father Madden's. He wasn't telling tales out of school. "Father Madden wasn't a priest yet. Neither he nor Bob Porter had been ordained. Bob never was."

Pascari's eyes filled with tears. "She took a friendship between two young men and turned it into a free-for-all. I don't think she ever cared for either of them. She was incapable of caring. That essential element was absent from her make-up...lovely packaging but nothing inside. Everyone she touched was left scarred. Everywhere she went she left heartache and humiliation.

I don't know if you can comprehend this Molly. Louise was *evil*. Really, I know you're thinking Pascari's gone bonkers. I had this little flirtation with this very young, very pretty woman and that because of guilt or some perversity I'm maligning this dead woman. At least that's what I might think if I heard this, but what I'm telling you is the truth! I wasn't surprised she was killed. No one seemed to be. If Louise inspired anything, it was surely that kind of senseless violence."

Pascari leaned back in his chair. He was not being charming or witty. He was not even attempting to defend himself. He was just trying to put things in perspective. He pulled forward, hunching over the desk.

"Molly, have you taken much philosophy or theology?"

"Not much, maybe nine credits in philosophy, maybe twelve in theology. I'm partial to theology." She smiled. It was ironic to Molly that she aced her theology courses, but barely made C's in her major.

"Do you believe that a person can be evil?" This seemed a bit too metaphysical for Molly's taste, but Doc was going somewhere that Molly had asked him to go. She respected him too much not to try and tag along.

"I don't know." It was an honest answer. She had thought about it, but it scared her. Free will, guilt, evil, grace, sin, all of it. They were moral icebergs and life was the Titanic. One thing was sure. Somebody had killed Nancy and that was wrong, but she couldn't quite say it was evil. Maybe it was all semantics. Right at that moment she was beginning to panic. Was Pascari suddenly going to grow pointed ears and a tail? Had she stumbled into some Faustian dream? She tried to focus. She was going off again and she needed to concentrate on what Doc was saying instead.

"I didn't." he stated. "I couldn't believe that anyone was completely evil. I thought that kind of thinking belonged with gypsies or Puritanic fundamentalists or, I'm not quite sure, but not to me. I was too rational, too intellectual to believe such nonsense. I was certain that no person could be evil and I figured if perchance someone were evil, if evil did exist in man, then that person would look the part, but Louise was and she didn't. Even if you don't believe me, Molly and I don't see how you could, Louise was evil personified." He sighed. "She was so beautiful and everything she touched she destroyed. My God, she was the Devil incarnate!"

Who was this? Doc was practically frothing at the mouth. If this is what even the memory of Louise Porter did to people, perhaps he was right. Molly had imagined Louise as troubled, but not bad, certainly not evil. Did Pascari think Louise was possessed? Okay, apparently Louise was not "a nice girl" but evil seemed over the top. Why had she married Bob Porter? Was it to prove that she had greater power than the Church? Did she love him, even a little? Doc was right about one thing. Molly couldn't grasp this.

Pascari shook his head. He placed his hands on the desk in front of him, open, palms upwards.

"Everything, everyone broken. This place has never been the same. With the exception of Bob Porter, everyone was relieved when she died". He saw the shock on Molly's face.

"Molly, it's not that anyone really wanted her dead. We just wanted her to go away. When nothing came of the investigation after her murder, people did their best to heal their wounds and move on. Now, twenty years later, she's somehow connected with the murder of another student. Louise Porter was and manages to remain a curse on this University. Is that the story you were after, Miss Monaghan?"

Cold. Molly could feel the cold in the small of her back. She could feel the cold in the words that had been spoken and in the speaker of those words. She believed Doc. She didn't want to think that Louise Porter had been evil. No matter what she did or didn't do. She was killed and her unborn child was killed. She didn't deserve that. Did Pascari think Nancy was evil, too? What did he think of Molly now? She wasn't sure. Was she in danger now from this man she revered? She couldn't believe that. Her head hurt. She wanted to give this up and go home. She wanted to leave and never come back. She didn't want to look at Pascari anymore.

She didn't want to be in this office, surrounded by all his awards and degrees and pictures. Where was the picture of Louise? Where was some remembrance of the woman for which he would have admittedly surrendered every shred of respectability and honor?

"Yes. That's it, at least part of it." Molly said quietly. "Thank you."

"Miss Monaghan," Pascari said, as he stood to walk her to the door, ever the gentleman, even now. "You could write a better story about Miss Kiernan than this. You could write about her talent and her friendship. Take the high road. Don't be foolish." he warned.

Kevin was waiting for her outside.

"That took forever. Any conclusions?" he asked.

"Yeah., but none about who murdered Nancy." Molly wanted to cancel or at least postpone the other appointments. She needed to talk this over with Kevin. Did he believe in evil? Could he make sense of the Louise Porter story as related by Joseph Patrick Pascari, Ph.D.? Maybe they could discuss it tonight, after all the interviews were over and they were sitting quietly waiting for someone to kill her. Maybe no one would come after her and she could call Mr. Reardon and go home and tell him everything. She could give the tapes to him. It was wishful thinking. She had thought of this less than brilliant plan, so she had to finish it. Two done and two to go. One really, since Father Madden was scheduled for the evening. There would be a break. There would be time to rest a little, perhaps to have something to eat. Later tonight they would listen to the new tapes, Molly's, not Nancy's. Then Kevin and she would try and piece together all of the puzzle. There was no time now. Now they walked together, silently, across campus to the Housing Office.

CHAPTER XIV

Molly looked over at Miss Kuyper and wanted nothing so much as something wonderfully cold and terribly alcoholic. She wondered if when this charade finally ended, there might not be a twelve step program in her future, providing, of course she had a future. She figured that this kind of thinking stemmed from the fact that, at that moment, she felt more than a little ridiculous. Polly's office looked like a sitting room in a Jane Austen novel. The vestiges of Christmas had not yet been swept away. A large ceramic Christmas Tree stood lit upon filing cabinet. A wreath with a slightly frayed plaid bow sat in the corner. Polly had banished any of the typical grey metal furniture that inhabited other university offices and replaced it with sturdy oak pieces that served the same purposes Two large, floral patterned armchairs were set off to the side of the room, where they were bathed in light from a nearby window. There was a round coffee table between the two chairs and in the center of the table what looked to be an antique silver tea set. Two delicate china cups and saucers rested on either side of the tea set. There was also a large plate of cookies whose fresh baked smell was guaranteed to disarm even the most cynical of souls. Miss Kuyper greeted Molly happily.

"Miss Monaghan, please let me take your coat and sit down, won't you?"

Molly thought it would make a quaint children's book. Polly and Molly have tea. She could envision the illustration of the room. Her caricature could sip her tea and then politely say (in a slightly Southern drawl, for all ladies sharing afternoon tea must speak in either a clipped British accent or a Southern drawl) "Miss Polly, this tea is just delicious. By the way, do you recall recently viciously attacking and killing my friend Miss Nancy Kiernan, of the Albany Kiernans?"

On the back of Molly's chair was a hand crocheted afghan. Now, if the victims had been killed with crochet hooks, then Molly might be onto something. Basically though there was something inherently wrong with the concept of this woman as a suspect and the more Molly played it out mentally, the more absurd the entire idea appeared to her.

What made her most uncomfortable was the fact that much more than any other factor, the reason Polly had made the final cut, was that she had suffered a breakdown. A little voice inside said that you didn't suspect someone of murder simply because she'd experienced some emotional problems. Polly had been treated for whatever ailed her. The killer more than likely had not considered himself sick. Still, it was necessary to go through the motions.

Polly poured Molly a cup of tea from a silver teapot and served it to her in a cup of bone china.

"This is lovely." Molly said genuinely. "You didn't have to do this, but I really appreciate it. I've never been in your office before. It's very welcoming."

I try to make it as homey as possible. I spend a lot of time here, so I like to make sure there are a few amenities. And don't forget, this is housing. Occasionally, a girl has some trouble with her roommate or maybe there's a financial issue. I never forget that you girls are far from home and that unfortunately the dorms seem more like barracks than bedrooms. The new dorms are much nicer." she said smiling. Molly's dorm had, in fact, been built as barracks. Soldiers returning from WWII had been housed there while they were earning their degrees courtesy of the GI Bill. Nancy's dorm was nicer, but it too was basically a no-frills set-up. The new dorms, at least the plans for them, looked palatial to most St. Anthony students. Molly suspected a hefty hike in tuition would follow on the heels of the new building. She didn't really care. At least the new buildings gave her an excuse to interview Polly.

"Miss Kuyper, won't the new dorms put an added strain on the Housing Department?" Molly sat, pen poised. She dutifully produced a notebook and pen. She realized at that moment, that she had failed to do that in the other two interviews. Suddenly she worried that may have been a serious mistake,

"Of course not! If anything, they will provide St. Anthony with much needed dormitory space. We have frequently had to turn students away due to a lack of housing availability." Polly replied.

Molly smiled. That was the party line. Enrollment was down a little from the glory days of previous years. The new dorms were being built to attract more students.

"How safe will the new dorms be?" Molly asked quietly.

I beg your pardon?"

"In light of the recent murder of Nancy Kiernan, a few people have begun to question the security at St. Anthony." Molly said flatly.

"I should think you would address that question to Security. Miss Kiernan's death has no relevance to housing." Miss Kuyper replied, her voice climbing.

"Someone ransacked her room. Doesn't that make you a little concerned?"

"That matter is being looked into, but we believe that it is most certainly an isolated incident. Miss Kiernan's death was unfortunate, indeed, quite tragic, but even the law agency involved in the investigation doubts whether there is any need to be concerned about overall safety here at the college." Molly could feel the interview slipping away. She had to change her approach, if she was going to get any information from Polly. She needed to shift gears now. Okay kid, she thought, time to step back and punt.

"Perhaps I'm over-reacting, but I was close to Nancy and her death has had an enormous effect on me." Molly hesitated. Then she almost whispered, "I can't believe it happened at St. Anthony. This place has always seemed so safe to me, almost sacred."

Polly Kuyper leaned forward.. Her voice was soft and comforting. "These things happen, Molly. You have to learn to pick up the pieces. No matter how difficult it may seem at this moment. You must put this behind you. You will get over this.

"Did you get over Louise Porter?" Buckle up, Molly thought. Here we go

"What?" Polly was not expecting this one. Her composure dissolved. Molly knew instinctively, it was time to start digging. It was time to open the old wounds. She wondered if she would ever feel clean after this ended. She feared she had become more than a little jaded.

"Nancy was working on the story of Louise Porter's murder. She had done some heavy-duty background work for the story. She mentioned to me, that you were close friends with Louise."

"That was a very long time ago." Polly said stiffly.

The tortoise was back in the shell. It was time for Molly to bleed a little. You give a little to get a little. You give a little more to get what you want. Maybe it was not such a bad idea to talk with Miss Kuyper after all. Maybe she could, in fact, help Molly resolve Nancy's death. Maybe all of that long ago pain and confusion had evolved into wisdom. There was only one way to find out.

"I didn't mean to revive painful memories. I just thought that if you were Louise's friend you would understand what's happening to me. I know it sounds a little strange, but it's the way I deal with overwhelming events in my life. I find somebody whom I trust and who has experienced something similar. I know that when my Dad died, I talked with friends who had also lost a parent. I formed something of a mourner's anonymous. It got me through." It was a lie. That's what had been recommended. Instead, Molly had taken long walks. For a little while, she had allowed herself to be pampered by friends and family. Then she had returned to school and to class, where there were few, if any reminders of her father. She had become friends with Father Tom Madden. It seemed that like Molly, he liked to roam the campus, in the very early, barely light hours of the morning. He would wave and she would return his wave. They established a kind of code. If either of them stopped and waited, then it was an unspoken invitation to walk together. Sometimes Tom would stop and sometimes Molly and sometimes neither. When they did walk together they talked about politics or sports or theology but never about death and never about her father.

Miss Kuyper was hooked. The obvious plea for counseling was the clincher. Every maternal instinct that had been hanging around rusting away rushed forward. No one had ever come to Polly Kuyper for anything but a room assignment. Molly had never heard of any girl seeking solace in this office. She doubted if many other students had ever been in it. Polly Kuyper had never mended others' wounds, either physical or emotional. She had not engaged in all nighters full of gossip and chocolate chip cookies. She had never wiped a child's eyes, hugged, kissed him and sent him on his way "all better". It showed. Polly loved St. Anthony and she loved the young people who made up its student body, but that love was not reciprocated. Most St. Anthony students seldom gave Miss Kuyper a thought. She was like the Post Office clerk or the maintenance crew.

For the first time in twenty years, a student had opened up to Polly Kuyper and she was damned if she was going to back away from it. Polly took a deep breath and told her story.

"Okay, Molly. I'm not sure I can help very much. I have a feeling that your friendship with Nancy was very different than my relationship with Louise, but I can tell that you're in pain and if I can help I will." This is why people hate us, Molly thought. The way that we will do anything, lie or cheat or steal to get the almighty story. She had vowed never to be this person. How easy it had been. How vulnerable was the woman who was about to walk through hell, because she thought Molly needed her help.

"Well, you know, Molly, I've always been an old maid. It isn't true that if you're not married by the time you're a certain age you become a spinster. Some people are born to it. They don't know quite how to talk to men. They don't know how to talk to anyone. I was like that. When I was very young I read a great deal. I began to believe the stories. I thought someday, someone dashing would come along and sweep me off my feet. I was raised here at the college. I was surrounded by young people, predominantly young men. You would think that would have made me less awkward socially, but it seemed to work in reverse. I found a little corner, a place in myself where I could hide. My parents were older and they were very quiet, shy individuals who found my lack of friends acceptable. I dare say, preferable.

You can't imagine what my life was like. I would go to school in town. The bus would pick me up in the morning. My mother would have packed my lunch, always the same: an apple or some other fruit, a sandwich, money to buy milk. At school, I stayed to myself. The other children seemed boisterous. I guess they frightened me a little. I wasn't teased or bullied or anything. I was simply ignored." Molly thought of how different her childhood had been. She would have been one of those boisterous school mates.

"Oh, don't feel sorry for me. I was happy. My parents loved me and protected me. I knew all the faculty here. I had the run of the University as a child. It's a beautiful spot, isn't it? When I was about seven or so, a few of the Friars built a swing set for me behind our house. It was wonderful. I spent hours on the swings and slide. They built a tree house, as well. Sometimes I would go up there and read. It was a quiet life and I think a very different life, but it was a good life, too.

A Sleeping Dog

When I graduated from high school, luckily St. Anthony was accepting women and I was given a full scholarship. The problem was that I really didn't fit in here. It was ironic. In so many ways it was my home. The girls who came here were more outgoing and assertive than I was. They viewed me as something of an oddity.

Then I met Louise. She was everything I wasn't, beautiful and witty. She could reduce the most sophisticated man to a blithering idiot, but she was lonely too. She sought me out. I was flattered by her attention. I needed a friend badly. I thought that was what Louise needed also. The rest of the girls seemed to ignore her or worse than that, they were openly hostile to her. At first I thought it was jealousy on their part but after I began to get to know Louise that opinion changed. It must have been their instinct for self-preservation that made people shy away from Louise."

Polly sipped her tea, then continued. "Louise used me. Because I had grown up here, I naturally had some influence with the staff. I could introduce Louise to the people she wanted to know. I could do favors for her and find others who would also do favors for her. I didn't mind. I was happy to do it. "I'd say 'You know my friend Louise wondered if you could…' I liked saying it, the words, my friend. I think I would have done anything for her.

Louise held no real affection for me. I realized that when my parents died. They passed away within six months of one another. I was devastated. It was the beginning of my senior year. More than anything else, I needed the comfort of a friend. Louise treated me badly. Cruelly. She would laugh about my being an old maid. She ridiculed me in front of others. More than that she seemed determined to destroy everyone and everything that was decent around her. It isn't fair, I know, to speak ill of the dead, but you have to understand about Louise." Polly was quiet then, strangely quiet. It is hard to travel back to dissect people and relationships. It is foreign to the spirit to force yourself to make that bizarre journey. Memories are one thing, but dragging out the heartache, the painful moments you would rather forget, that is quite another. Molly kept the silence. This was Polly's tale and she would allow Polly to tell it in her own good time. Miss Kuyper looked quite small at that moment. Polly Kuyper was not small, not physically. but just at that moment, Molly could envision the lonely little girl, swinging as high and as hard as she could, the child sitting by herself reading page after page of worlds full of adventure and excitement, the dutiful daughter who would have been the most faithful of friends. Could she have been hurt enough twenty years ago to take a knife to Louise?

"I'm sorry, I seem to have lost track of things. You wanted to know how I felt when Louise was killed, didn't you? "Molly just nodded.

"Strangely enough I took Louise's death very badly. Perhaps it was because of the timing. It was after all, not long after both of my parents passed away. Also there was the manner of her death. It was very violent and I think that had an enormous effect on me. More than anything else, I think it may have been that we had grown apart. I had more or less given up on our friendship. Louise's behavior, that I had always made efforts to excuse, had begun to disgust me. Then suddenly she was dead. You know, Miss Monaghan that it is common for people to think that if you love someone and then that person is suddenly lost to you, your grief is unconsolable. But it's not. If you've stopped loving someone and then that person dies, that is when your grief is unconsolable. I became quite ill after Louise's death, so ill that I ..." Polly stopped. She was searching for the right words. Molly knew that Miss Kuyper was deciding whether or not to trust her.

"I was so ill," she continued, "that I required treatment. I went to a hospital in Minnesota. It is not common knowledge. It's important to me that people here at the college not know of my illness. Somehow your friend Nancy found out about it. She probably already told you about it." Molly shook her head. "No," she said defiantly, "Nancy was not like that.

She didn't gossip. Whatever she found out about you or anyone else she kept to herself." That was true. It wasn't Nancy's fault that Kevin and Molly knew Miss Kuyper's secrets. It was whoever murdered Nancy.

"Well, that says something for her ethics, at least."

"It's probably what got her killed." Molly said wryly. "But she covered herself. She got tapes."

"What are you talking about?" Polly demanded.

"I think that Nancy was killed because she unearthed some kind of evidence from the Louise Porter murder. If that's the case then, the killer is probably someone that Nancy interviewed." Molly explained.

"What tapes are you talking about? Nancy Kiernan interviewed me and she most certainly did not tape record that interview."

"I'm afraid you're wrong. Nancy carried a portable recorder in her purse. She never did an interview she didn't tape."

Mis Kuyper looked panicked, "If that's true, then wouldn't whoever went through Nancy's room have stolen or destroyed those tapes?"

"Nancy had already given them to me. I never played the tapes and don't have any intention of doing so. It's frankly none of my business. But I will have to hand them over to the police. They might somehow lead the police to Nancy's killer."

Miss Kuyper went pale. "Miss Monaghan, if you have one shred of decency you'll destroy those tapes. I don't know who else Nancy interviewed, so I don't have any idea how many lives could be ruined if they are made public. I do know that it will most assuredly ruin everything I've worked for over the past twenty years. I know my reputation as an old maid here at the college and I can live with that. I won't be able to sustain the whispers, the accusations, the innuendo, that will abound, if people find out I was treated for a nervous disorder. I'm not worried about my job, that's secure. But I won't be able to stay here. I'm not strong. Some people are but I'm not. St. Anthony is my home. It's my family. It's my life."

Molly had never imagined an occasion where she would witness Polly Kuyper in tears, but one had arisen. Miss Kuyper had covered her face with her hands and she was rocking slowly back and forth, muttering: "Please, please don't. Please don't. It's all I have. It's all I've ever had." Molly stared at the floor. Her eyes hurt when she looked at Miss Kuyper. How could Nancy have done this to someone? For what? Do you pull the emotional rug out on people for the rather inglorious pursuit of a story for your journalism class? Molly was ashamed. She wasn't any better than Louise. She too had preyed on Polly Kuyper. She had lied and betrayed her.

"Miss Kuyper, I didn't realize. You're probably right. Maybe it would be best to destroy the tapes. At any rate, I won't do anything right away. It's just that if the tapes are important ... Look, I promise that I'll give it some time. Everything you've said to me is absolutely confidential, really. And I won't give the police the tapes right away. Who knows, maybe they'll get Nancy's killer without ever hearing the tapes. If that happens you have my word that the recordings will be destroyed. Okay? Miss Kuyper, are you okay?"

She didn't answer. She just continued to cry. Molly left the office without good-byes. She doubted that Miss Kuyper was even aware of her exit.

"Well?" Kevin asked.

"Kevin, do we have any Irish whiskey at home?" Molly asked quietly.

"I think so, but I've never seen you drink whiskey. Did the interview go that badly?"

"Worse. Oh Christ, Kevin, It's so bad. It's all so bad." Molly was in the thick of this now. She couldn't go back. She couldn't unsay what she had said or heal the wounds she had opened, quiet the fear and anger she had unleashed. This was why Nancy had looked the way she did in the dining hall that last night. It was that the truth took no prisoners. What fools they were, both she and Nancy. It was the era of Watergate, the heroic age of Bernstein and Woodward. Journalism students were inspired. They dreamt of Pulitzer Prizes and book deals and their bylines on articles that "exposed the soft underbelly of corruption." No one spoke of this, the two edged sword of truth, the look in the eyes of those whose guilt was suddenly held up to the scrutiny of the public. Okay. She needed to stop whining. She would go back to Kevin's and shower and change and have a stiff drink. She would bolster her courage and see this thing through.

"Maybe you should have something to eat before your 'confession' with the good Father?"

"No. I've lost my appetite and greatly increased my thirst."

Kevin put his arm around her. "I'll pour." More than this Molly could not hope for. More than this was beyond reason. There is nothing better than a handsome man who would double as both a good friend and bartender. Well, maybe there was one thing better. She wished that was what she was preparing to confess later that evening.

CHAPTER XV

Molly slipped the portable recorder into her purse. She was breaking all the rules. Kevin told her he would wait for her outside the Friary. Even if Father Madden were the killer, he wasn't about to try anything inside. Kevin would wait in the shadows, some distance away. Molly would talk with the last of the suspects while Kevin waited in the car.

He watched Molly enter the side portico of the Friary where Tom Madden was already waiting for her. Molly followed Tom into one of the little sitting rooms beside the chapel. She nonchalantly reached in her purse and pressed the record button on the recorder. He sat across from her. dressed and ready for her sins, clad in the brown robes of St. Francis and the purple stole of repentance. Molly began the ritual: "Bless me Father, for I have sinned. It has been six months since my last confession." Molly always began the same way. The words she had learned in the beginning. She would not be robbed of them. There had been too many Saturday afternoons, with her chin scraping the hand rest and her knees digging into the kneeler, in the dark, wooden closet of a confessional. It was necessary then to number your sins. She would think "I dishonored my mother and my father fifty times, well, maybe forty. I wished to do bodily harm to my brother a hundred times (but alas, he was too fast for me.)" --Long ago confessions, full of earnest penitence. Some of the regret, some of the repentance remained, never more than now - when she prepared for a confession that might not be her own.

"I've lied." Molly said quietly. (She had given up the numbers.)

Tom waited. Molly cleared her throat. "I lied about Nancy's death."

Tom Madden looked puzzled, but he remained silent. A lifetime of training had taught him to give the sinner time. Time to reflect, time to explain, time to get it all out.

"I've lied to you about Nancy. I've been investigating her death. I have all her resource material on the death of Louise Porter."

"All what materials?" he asked.

"Taped interviews, notes and some other stuff… things I should have gone to the police with. I was afraid to, but now I think it's time that people learned the truth."

"Molly, do you know the truth?" he asked.

"I can guess.

"Really? You didn't come to confess to me tonight, did you?"

"Yes, Father"

"Oh, no Father! You came to get me to confess. You came to accuse. Do you think I killed Louise Porter?" Molly tried to remain calm. She had never seen Tom angry. His mammoth jaw was quivering and he looked like he wanted to reach over and beat Molly.

"I don't know, Father. There are certain indications…

"*Certain indications*? "Molly, this is me. Have you lost your mind entirely? Certain indications? What did you expect to happen tonight? Did you expect me to ask your forgiveness, to confess to murder, like some dime-store villain? To fall on my knees and weep and say 'Yes I did it and I'm glad to be free, after twenty years, I'm glad to be free!?"

"No, I guess not."

"Well, you're friend Nancy did. She had the audacity to come here, full of theories and rumors, best left forgotten."

"Theories about who fathered Louise Porter's baby?" The color drained from his face. They would never need a blood test for this one. Here was Mr. Paternity. The great Sin - the biggee. The rest were all venial by comparison. Molly thought a giant red "A" would appear on his forehead momentarily.

"Molly, do you realize how many lives could be ruined by releasing that kind of information?" Goddamn him, Molly thought. He's concerned about his career. At least Pascari had cared about the girl.

"What about the lives already ruined? Lives that have been taken -- Louise's, Nancy's your baby's? Tell me the value of their lives, Father." All of the doubt and guilt was gone. There was only anger.

"You're very good, Molly. They could have used you at the Inquisition." He sank in the chair and began to mumble: "Louise Porter *was* carrying my child. At least she said it was mine but you couldn't always count on what Louise said. I don't know what you know, Molly or what you think you know. What is it that you want from me exactly?"

"I want to know what happened. I want to know your part in all of this"

"We were very young. I guess we didn't really know how young. Bob and I were about seventeen or eighteen years old when we entered the seminary. Nothing they taught us there prepared us for Louise. I didn't like her, really. I was attracted to her, a male hormone in a test tube would have been attracted to her. Bob, though, was crazy about her. I don't think she ever loved him but she could get to him.

I didn't worry about it at first. I figured it would pass. By the time Louise came into our lives, we were a few months from ordination and Bob was deeply religious. I loved God and all the rest of it. I did what I needed to do to get through, but Bob wasn't like that. He was the best person I ever met. He was so earnest. He loved completely, totally. He believed. Can you understand? Really believed. He was just perfect for Louise, custom-made. I thought, it'll pass. Years later, when we're having a couple of after dinner drinks, I'll get up in some restaurant and have the piano player play *Every Little Breeze Seems to Whisper Louise* and we'd have a good laugh over it. But he comes in one night and says to me,. 'I'm leaving. I'm in love and I'm going to marry the girl.' How could anybody be that stupid?

We fought that night. Fists. We went out in the yard behind the Friary, like a couple of school kids and nearly killed one another. I remember I said he didn't have to marry her to get what he wanted. Plenty of other guys hadn't. You should have seen his face then. I see it. I see it often. I loved him. I really loved him, not in a sexual way, but as something I could never even aspire to be. You see, Bob was the only person I have ever met who was totally guiltless. He was good. The boy was so good and he was packing it in for this girl who was using him. He couldn't see it. He thought he was lucky." They were silent then. Molly was listening so intently that she could hear the distance in the priest's words. She could hear the pain and the struggle.

"I had sex with Louise. I didn't lust after her and I didn't love her. I had to prove to myself that Bob had made a bad bargain. Bob made bad choices in friends and in lovers. I was cruel to the girl. I'm more ashamed of that than anything. I was so obsessed with proving how unfaithful she was, how low a person she was, I got right down there with her. That was the only thing between us. My anger and arrogance, my cruelty to her. The nastier I was to her, the more she managed to find time to be with me. She cheated on Bob and I cheated on the Church and that's all we were a couple kids getting even.

We didn't like ourselves and we didn't like each other. We were perfectly matched. What is it you always say, Moll?" Then he laughed a little, derisive laugh and it was worse than sobbing. God punished me. I decided to give it up. You know, repent and be saved. I had gone home to be with my parents. I was preparing for ordination. I don't know. I saw myself for what I was and finally, I found my anchor. I came home to my God. I confessed and repented. For the first time in my life, I got it.

So much of the theology I had taken was on an intellectual plane. I had never really felt the love and grace of God and then I looked in some moral mirror and was appalled by what I saw there. I went home for awhile, to just go home, to be away from here. I needed to feel clean again, but mostly to figure out what I was doing and how I could stop doing it. I prayed for forgiveness and grace and strength. By then, Louise had gotten to me."

Molly remained still. She listened, reversing roles with the priest. It was as if she were at the theater or watching a movie. In those moments, she didn't think of Tom Madden as someone she knew as priest or a friend. He was a person with a story, a sad, sick, poignant, painful story. She heard it and she waited. She feared what she might hear but she needed to hear it..

Tom continued. "I get this call from Louise telling me she's pregnant with my child. I asked her how she knew it was mine and she laughed. She had this laugh that was terrifyingly cruel. She knew, she said. She was sure." Molly hated him at that moment. She hated him for his self-pity and his selfishness and most of all for his overwhelming stupidity. He looked at Molly then and saw that hatred. He saw the disappointment and the harsh judgment in her expression.

"Don't be so high-handed Molly. What I had done was wrong. I knew that but it was not some small problem. I was weeks away from ordination and months away from parenthood. Despite the low-esteem in which you may hold me, I wasn't the only person I was concerned about. I had already hurt Bob. She was married to him. I took my parents' car and came down here to St. Anthony. I thought maybe I could talk to Louise. I had to find out what she was going to do. I had to figure out what to do myself. I kept thinking what a sorry excuse I was for a human being and I kept imagining what Bob's face would look like when she told him. I was sure she would tell him. She wouldn't spare any details.

At the same time, I thought, I was going to be a father. I could have a child that was mine and so maybe something good would come out of all the bad. My own child, except I would never know for sure if it was mine. I tried to think of leaving the priesthood and marrying Louise. Maybe she loved me. Maybe I could learn to love her. I knew somewhere deep inside there would be no happy ending. I couldn't imagine that God would allow Louise to have a baby. What a life that child would have with Louise as a mother and if I were the father, strike two...

I have never been so frightened, so lost as when I arrived at Bob's house. I knew he would be at work. I would talk to Louise. I knew it would be better if I had a plan. I had none. Maybe she had some answers. I opened the screen door and walked in the kitchen. I looked down and she was there on the floor. I had never seen a corpse, at least not like that. I thought I was going to be sick, but instead I just ran. I ran back to my car and pushed that pedal to the floor and did eighty or ninety miles an hour until I was back in my parents' driveway. I went upstairs to the bathroom and I vomited. I wept and I vomited and I wanted to kill myself but I didn't have the guts. No guts. Big Tom Madden, the gutless wonder. I thought they would come and get me.

I thought the police would come and drag me away and all my sins would be public. I'd be tried for murder and I feared for myself, but also what it would do to my parents and Bob and the Church...

I didn't sleep or eat. I waited and worried, but no one came, nothing happened. Louise and I had been discreet in our sinning and as far as anyone knew, I was miles away when she was killed. I didn't go to her wake and funeral. I sent a sympathy card to Bob. He never responded. The police never even questioned me."

"There were rumors about you. I don't understand." Molly did understand, but she wished she didn't. It was a classic example of the hush-up power of the Church. What small town sheriff would take on Holy Mother Church? If Madden was at home, miles away, why hang out dirty laundry? There was also the economic side. What would the Louise Porter story have done to St. Anthony University? If the university folded, the town died. So, one troubled girl is killed and her murder goes unsolved, unnoticed. Bury the girl and the scandal and move on. Molly could feel her throat tighten. She tried to keep the bile from rushing upward.

"The police never knew I was there that day, but I was and I've remained there. I know. You think I should have come forward. When they didn't find anyone, maybe my information would have helped. I thought about it. I weighed the cost. Who would have paid the most for my sins? What would it have meant to Bob or to the University or my family?

They tell me that I'm wonderfully intellectual. People can't figure out where I get the time to read. I get plenty of time- time when I can't sleep, time when I am supposed to be meditating about something religious, but I'm picturing a young man's face instead or I'm opening a screen door and witnessing Hell. I'm remembering a summer day when I saw a girl who had lain in the same bed with me, a beautiful girl, in pieces on a kitchen floor. I'm meditating on what it means to be a coward. I'm remembering that every day and every day it takes more Scotch for me to exhibit the famous Madden charm, charm that comes from hiding, from running.

"Why did you become a priest?" Molly asked. "You could have run from that, too."

"I wondered about that. On the day of my ordination, when everyone thought I was this splendid young man dedicating myself to God and His Church, sacrificing myself out of love and idealism, I knew what I was. I was a coward and an adulterer, running to God, because I didn't know where else to run.

I have been a good priest, Molly. Maybe that's because I know the price of guilt. You know that. I listen to others' sins and I find them easy to forgive. They do not seem so great in comparison to my own. I welcome the opportunity to care for people and to share their guilt and to counsel them. I tell them of God's mercy and I wonder if I can begin to believe in it myself. I work and I pray and I reach out in the hope that maybe a God who is so loving and so forgiving can forgive me. Maybe then someday I might be able to forgive myself."

They sat quietly and let the silence fill the room. It poured into the corners that had heard too much, it streamed down into the raw, aching crevices of their hearts. Molly was crying. She had not realized it, but now as she strained to look at him, she was forced to wipe the tears away. Tom handed her a handkerchief.

"What should I do?" Molly asked. Father Tom pulled his chair close to hers and took hold of her hands.

"Maybe I'm not the person to answer that question."

"I think you are. Maybe you're the only person who can answer it." She meant it. She needed him to say, "Put it away. Louise's story has caused too much pain already." She needed counsel and advice and she needed it from Father Tom Madden. The Tom Madden who deserved absolution, who had done his penance.

Tom sighed. "Molly, you have an intuitive morality. I would be hard-put to argue with it. Do whatever you feel needs to be done, but please be careful."

"I go to the police with this, you have a lot to lose. These are different times. This time they might come for you. You might get arrested or worse." She feared that maybe this might break him. What if he were arrested? Even if he wasn't convicted, it would be a mess. What would it do to St. Anthony? What would it do to him personally? Maybe he too would have a car accident.

"I lost the really important things a long time ago." He smiled. "Don't worry. I'm a survivor. Others will suffer, though. Molly, you need to understand that. There will be many people hurt by all of this. I tried to explain that to Nancy Kiernan, but you know how effective that was. Do whatever you think is right and I'll stand behind you, but weigh the consequences of your actions."

"I have one more thing for you to lose, Father." Molly reached in her purse and handed him the recorder. "I think the erase button works fairly well, but you may want to try it out." It took a few minutes to register. Then Father Madden took the recorder and placed it on the table. He walked Molly to the side portico. He brushed the hair from her eyes and kissed her softly on the forehead. He made the Sign of the Cross above her head and whispered: "May the Lord bless and keep you. May he make His sun to shine upon you and turn His countenance toward you." Then he turned away and walked toward the sitting room. Molly turned her collar to the cold and started toward the car.

CHAPTER XVI

It was over. Molly had dragged herself through an emotional landmine and she was finished with it. It wasn't worth it. She had been right in the beginning. Nancy would still be dead and Louise would still be dead and all the pain and dirt that had been kicked up would remain long after the reasons for kicking it up had been forgotten. She had lost her anger, her outrage. She would still mourn Nancy. She would still miss her, but she couldn't put these people through any more suffering. She ticked off the names on the list: Sutton, Kuyper, Madden, Doc – all of them, facing the mirror every morning, putting their heads on their pillows at night, each with fear and shame and secrets as his or her constant companions, each battling his or her, heretofore private, demons. It was possible that one of them was also a murderer. Possible, but not certain, not even now could Molly know which, if any of them, had been desperate enough to have killed.

Kevin would be pleased. He had never been enthusiastic about any of this. Molly could move back to her dorm room. It might seem somewhat sterile now. She would miss Kevin, however much she hated to admit that. She had never been totally at home in the dorm. She easily tired of giggles and screams and a hundred other girls who frequently looked like they were cloned. It wasn't that she didn't like the girls, there were just too many people the same age and the same gender in the same place. It had been good to be alone away from campus. It was better to be with Kevin.

Speaking of Kevin, where was he? It wasn't like him not to be here. Maybe he miscalculated the time. He could have gone for coffee, but that didn't make sense. He was too cautious for that. He would never leave her alone, not tonight of all nights, not here of all places. He said he would hang back a little. He would be out of sight in case the killer decided to make his move. Kevin had been right. This was not smart. What if he's not somewhere just out of my sight, Molly thought? What if I'm somewhere just out of his sight?

Then another thought, an even less pleasant thought occurred to Molly. What if Kevin wasn't around, because the killer had found him first? That had never occurred to her. Neither of them had thought about who might be watching the watcher. All those horror movies, where you think the police officer is waiting in the car, guarding the house and then there's the quick shot of him dead behind the steering wheel just as the killer opens the door.

A Sleeping Dog

What if the hunted had successfully switched places with the hunter? She thought about going back to the Friary and asking Tom to take her home. Molly began to walk faster. I've got to get this all behind me. I've got to get Kevin and go home and forget it, bury it. Molly tried not to hear the quickening of steps behind her. She tried to avoid the arm that grabbed at her and she uttered: "Please no", as she felt the first brush of the blade against her skin.

Molly was in a cold, dark place. She was far away but she could hear her name. Someone was calling to her. She ran toward the sound, but her legs weren't moving. The sound was getting louder. The first person she saw was Kevin. He was standing over her. Someone was holding her hand. She turned to look at who it was. It hurt to turn her head. She remembered the blade then. She remembered the slash. She stared at Father Madden, but she couldn't speak. He smiled down at her. Where in the hell was she? Was she dreaming? Had she died? Kevin spoke first. "You fainted." Molly tried to shake her head, but that hurt too much. Kevin laughed, "Yeah, I know you don't faint. It's not in your contract. Well you passed out then, does that sound better?" Molly spoke then. "Who?"

"I hate to admit it, but you picked it. Polly Kuyper. I wasn't the only one waiting for you. I called Jerry Reardon the other day and he's been following us all day. He thought your plan was stupid at best, but he figured it would be better to guard you than to talk to you. I was in my car and he was in his. We noticed somebody hanging around the Friary. At first, I thought it was just a jogger or somebody making a late visit, but then when that person seemed to hiding in the shadows I figured we were in trouble.

We watched as you left the Friary, but we lost sight of you for a minute. The next thing we know, we see you get grabbed from behind. We didn't know it was Polly. She had this St. Anthony jacket on with the hood pulled over her face. She was wearing jeans and she looked like a guy. We didn't know it was a woman. Not that it would have made much difference. You wouldn't believe how strong she is. We got her anyway, but not before she got a quick one in on you… Molly was trying to comprehend it all. She couldn't believe that Kevin was still talking. He had said more in the last five minutes than she had heard him utter in the previous four years. It didn't matter what he said. He was there. Kevin was there and he had protected her. She was safe. She looked over at Tom...Tom who had talked so much tonight, who had spoken painful truth and shameful memories. He stood beside her now, holding her hand, silently watching. She was lying in the infirmary and she was safe and two people she loved were beside her protecting her body and soul. She didn't care about Polly. She couldn't care, there wasn't anything left to care.

Molly had narrowly escaped death and she had been through a day that would haunt her forever. She was exhausted. She couldn't keep her eyes open. She couldn't hold on to consciousness. Molly slept. Right in the middle of Kevin's description of Polly's failed murder attempt, Molly fell sound asleep. She slept for two days. The doctors couldn't believe it. They had not even given her a sedative. She stayed in the infirmary

CHAPTER XVII

How had she gotten here? So far tonight, she had been wrestled to the ground, cuffed, arrested and fingerprinted. She had been strip searched, which had been humiliating. This was the part she had never considered. There would be a trial. No, there must not be a trial. The University must be spared that.

She sat motionless. There was a table with a few chairs. On the other side of the two way mirror, Sheriff Thompson conversed with Jerry Reardon.

"It's the damndest thing. Have you ever seen anything like this?" Thompson asked.

Reardon shook his head. "You know, mostly our homicides are more run of the mill. I've seen bloodier ones, but never anything stranger. She waived her right to an attorney?" Reardon didn't like that. This was going to be tricky enough. He figured, at the very least, they were going to need a psych eval. The Sheriff was definitely out of his depth. So far the suspect had said nothing. She had given her name and address and when she was read the Miranda warning, she simply said, "No, thank you. That won't be necessary." She had said it as if she were declining a cold drink or an easy chair. Since then she had sat at the table, smiling into the mirror, knowing full well she was being watched and appearing totally unaffected by the situation.

"Jerry, you've done a lot of these and I haven't done any. Would you mind questioning her? I'll just sit in." Jeff Thompson was a realist. His job as Sweet Valley Sheriff had taken him into court occasionally, but rarely had his testimony been scrutinized. He knew that a lot would be riding on this interrogation.

"It's not my case. Anyway I thought it was the state's purview because it happened on campus. Aren't the troopers coming for her?"

"They'll pick her up in the morning. I was really just going to book her and guard her until morning, but the captain suggested that I try to get a confession tonight. He said something about defendants getting less cooperative in the cold light of day, as opposed to having just gotten caught in the act. I mentioned you were here and might help me out."

Reardon knew he was stuck. The truth was as much as he didn't want to get involved in this, he was intrigued by Polly. He had seen more than his share of hoods and "homicidal maniacs" but this one, this one was different. Thompson was right.

"Okay, but I can't promise anything and you better make some coffee. This is going to be a long night."

When the two men walked into the room, Polly stared at Jerry Reardon and her smile vanished. "I don't know you. You're the man that grabbed me on campus. Who are you?" She asked. There was no hostility or animosity in her voice, just curiosity.

"My name is Lieutenant Reardon and I'm a homicide detective. I kept you from killing Molly Monaghan tonight and held you so that Sheriff Thompson could arrest you for that murder attempt. You realize that you are charged with that murder and the murder of Nancy Kiernan and very likely you will also be charged with the murder of Louise Porter."

"That was a very long time ago." Polly interrupted.

"There's no statute of limitations on murder, Miss Kuyper. Louise Porter's murder is still an open case." Reardon was polite and formal in his statement. There was no portrayal of emotion. No hint of that one moment of terror when he realized that Molly was in danger and that he might have to tell Tess Monaghan that her daughter was dead and he could have, should have prevented it.

Reardon was good at hiding his emotions. In the interrogation room he was often more an actor than a cop. Early on in his career, he had come to the conclusion, that if he were to survive this job, then he had to be open to the perverse, the violent, the corrupt, the darkest side of society. He had to think like killers and rapists and thieves. He had to talk to them as he would his friends, without revealing his revulsion or disgust or pity or fear. He continued:

"These are very serious charges, Miss Kuyper. Are you aware of the gravity of your situation?"

"Yes" said Polly quietly.

"You'll note that we are going to discuss those charges, you and the sheriff and me and that we're going to tape record this discussion." Reardon nodded to Thompson, who started the tape and recorded the time, date and situation.

"I'" said Kuyper quietly.

"Pardon me?" Reardon asked.

"You've should have said 'you and the sheriff and I'." Polly said authoritatively.

Reardon smiled. "Of course, thank you. May we proceed, Miss Kuyper?"

Polly was touched by his courtesy. "Yes, Lieutenant." she replied politely.

"Now, you are aware that you are charged with murder and attempted murder and that you have the right to have your attorney present during questioning? In light of the seriousness of these charges, are you certain you wouldn't like to wait for your lawyer?"

Polly sounded annoyed. "For the third time, no, I don't want an attorney. I'm not an idiot. You don't need to continually repeat the same things. I know I have the right to an attorney and I also have the right not to have an attorney. It's my decision and I wish you would stop asking me about it."

Reardon smiled. This tape was like gold. The trooper was right. There was no time like the present to question this one.

"Miss Kuyper, did you follow Molly Monaghan earlier tonight? he asked.

"Yes, I believe you know I did."

"I do, but I don't know why and that's what I would like to know."

"I intended to kill her." Polly replied. Sheriff Thompson was stunned. She had said it like someone would say "I was going to see a movie" or "I was going to pick up my dry cleaning."

Even Reardon was surprised.

"Why?" he asked. If she were going to kill Molly because Molly could lead the police to her, then why this confession? It wasn't as if she was overcome with remorse or that she was overwhelmed by it all. She seemed perfectly calm, almost placid.

"I have my reasons." she stated calmly.

"Are those the same reasons you had for killing Nancy Kiernan?"

"Somewhat." Polly replied. Her face betrayed no emotion.

"Then you do admit that you killed Nancy Kiernan."

"Yes."

"How?"

"I would think you know that, too"

"Enlighten me."

"I'm very tired, Lieutenant. Is it really necessary to go through all this."

"Yes, Miss Kuyper, I'm afraid it is. You've confessed to a brutal murder and a murder attempt. The details are very important. Believe me, the Sheriff and I are also tired, but we need to know how and why." The motive, they needed a motive. He thought he knew it, but now all bets were off. Now he wanted to know what made this woman tick.

"Yes, that makes sense. I'm sorry for this mess, really I am. I'll tell you how. Do you think I might have a cup of tea? I'm parched."

"Certainly, would you like anything to eat?" This "coddling" of suspects was derided by some of the older, seemingly tougher interrogators but Reardon had witnessed its efficacy on more than one occasion. As his mother used to say "You get more flies with honey than you do with vinegar."

"No thank you, Lieutenant. It's very kind of you to offer." She smiled.

"Now Miss Kuyper, can you explain, in detail how you murdered Nancy Kiernan?" he asked.

"I'm not sure where to begin."

"Start on the night of December 18th. That was the night Nancy Kiernan was murdered." That night, Reardon remembered, he was Christmas shopping with his daughter. She was about the same age as

Molly, which meant she was about the same age as Nancy. He tried not to think about it. He tried to keep his life compartmentalized. That seemed to be increasingly difficult, the older his children became. He focused on the woman across from him. She had to be his only thought now. Why? He needed to know why.

"I had followed Nancy for a few nights. I was waiting for an opportunity to avail itself, but she was seldom alone. I almost went home, when she got in the car with Kevin O'Connor, but then, when they didn't drive off immediately, I waited. Before long, Nancy got out of the car and Kevin drove away. There's a tree lined pathway from the parking lot to Nancy's dorm. I waited for her there. I stood behind one of the trees. As she walked past, I called her name. She turned toward me and I stabbed her to death." Jeff Thompson was in shock. Nothing had prepared him for this.

"Did Nancy struggle?" Reardon asked. It was hard to tell from the autopsy. He hoped she had fought.

"Not really. I think she was too shocked and the knife was heavy and sharp. I think she was very much weakened by the first thrust of the blade." she explained. He had questioned a number of suspects who had stabbed their victims. Not until this moment, had one described the "thrust" of the weapon. More than the murder, the manner and vocabulary of this woman, was unnatural and disconcerting.

"And is this the same knife you stabbed Miss Monaghan with tonight?"

"Yes, it's the same knife, but I wasn't sure I actually was able to stab Molly. She seemed to duck out of the way and then, it seemed like Mr. O'Connor and you wrestled the knife from me. Was Miss Monaghan seriously hurt?"

"Not seriously, no. She'll be alright" he added "She'll be able to testify" Then something occurred to him.

"Miss Kuyper, the knife you used tonight and that you used to kill Nancy Kiernan, have you ever used that knife before in the commission of any other crimes?"

Polly stared at Reardon. Who was he? How did he know? She looked at the blank face of Jeff Thompson. Somehow, this man knew. What else did he know? He had said "testify." Molly would be well enough to testify. That couldn't happen. She had given up so much. She had given her very soul to save the University from this and now all the dirty laundry would be aired. Louise would win at last. This could not be allowed.

Polly looked him directly in the eyes.

"You know." She said and for the first time, fear even desperation crept into her voice. Reardon nodded. "Yeah, I know, but say it."

"Miss Kuyper," he asked, almost gently, "Do you need me to repeat the question?" Polly shook her head.

"The knife was used many years ago in the commission of another crime." There was a pause and Jerry Reardon knew what was coming. He waited. Then Polly said clearly, "I used that knife to kill Louise Porter in the summer of 1956."

"Are there any other crimes you've committed with that or any other weapon?"

Polly smiled. "Forgive me, Father, for these sins and all the sins of my past life? Isn't that how it goes?"

"Not everybody does that line." Reardon had been taught to say that at the end of confession. He had asked a teacher, "What happens if I forget a sin? Does that mean I've made a bad confession? The "all the sins of my past life" was the clincher, it covered everything.

"No, Lieutenant, there are no other crimes connected with that knife or me." She liked Lieutenant Reardon, from God knows where, who had brought her to this moment of confession. She wished she could explain to him alone, why she had been compelled to do what she had done. She believed that he could understand that the sacrifice of the few for the many was necessary, though brutal.

She would not. She had fought the good fight and would not now forfeit whatever victory had been and might still be achieved at so great a cost. Only she knew how truly evil Louise was and what that demon had planned. Polly had given everything, even her soul, surrendering not only her future but her hereafter by assuming the role of both soldier and executioner. She wanted to explain, but would not trade her sacrifice for…for what? For understanding? For clemency? For forgiveness?

"Lieutenant, I am very tired. Could we continue this in the morning?" She looked tired. She looked weary and sad but not frightened or remorseful. Polly Kuyper seemed strangely calm, even peaceful, like a climber at the summit of a mountain or a marathon runner at the finish line.

"I won't ask you any other questions tonight, Miss Kuyper. I will ask you to write your confession on this paper, including as much as you remember about the details. When you've signed it, the sheriff will escort you to your cell where you can get some sleep. Thank you for your cooperation." He could have pressed forward, but she was finished for tonight. He would let her drink her tea and write her confession. In the morning, the troopers would come and she would become their problem. Reardon knew there would be lengthy phone interviews and depositions, but he doubted if there would be a trial. Maybe. Maybe a defense attorney could convince Polly to plead diminished capacity or insanity, but that was just as likely as Reardon being drafted into the Bolshoi Ballet.

This woman, who looked harmless even fragile after this long night, this woman was granite. She sought nothing from her captors. She gave nothing. He had to talk to Molly and ask her what she thought. What had made this woman kill and do so without remorse? "In cold blood" was the phrase that came to mind, but somehow that didn't fit. Reardon believed that she had done what she considered necessary, what was expedient. Originally, he had expected tears, maybe rants, even voices, "I was commanded by God…I couldn't stop the voices…." Maybe a shot of paranoia, "They were after me, they would never have left me alone, I had to do it." He had expected a madman, (he knew it was sexist, but he hadn't really considered a woman suspect) or a fanatic. Instead he found himself questioning a slightly frumpy, middle-aged woman who, no matter what he knew or what she said, he couldn't quite believe would harm anyone.

Enough. He said goodbye to Sheriff Thompson and the deputy. He'd stop by the campus infirmary on the way home and check up on Molly.

Maybe Tess was there by now and they'd share a cup of coffee. He had a long ride home and it was already late. He'd call Kevin O'Connor in the morning and see how he was doing. Nobody in this case turned out to be the way Molly had presented them. Kevin was a nervous wreck. Although, Jerry thought, "What would I have been like in his shoes?" The suspect in the murder of your girlfriend and another friend likely to be the next victim, all this when you're barely twenty-one? Reardon wondered how Molly had gotten Kevin to go along with it all. He smiled. She had inherited her mother's gift. He had known Tess Monaghan to attain very generous donations from men so tight that, as his mother used to say, "They wouldn't give a dime to see Christ ride a bicycle." He, himself, had fallen prey to Tess. He couldn't count the number of Church Carnivals or school bazaars, where he had labored long and hard, for a smile and a heartfelt "You're the best. I don't know what we'd do without you."

This too, this very troubling, baffling case, there had been not a moment's hesitation in taking it on. When he heard Tess' voice on the phone, the concern and the fear, there wasn't anything he wouldn't have done for her. He was glad of his part in this. He had saved Molly's life. That rarely happened in his job. Jerry Reardon was used to picking up the pieces. He didn't like to think about how many times he had to look into the eyes of parents and tell them the worst things a human being can hear.

A Sleeping Dog

He didn't like to think of it, but he did. More and more, as he watched his daughter leave the house for a concert or to go to the show, he was haunted by the ghastly visions that he could not erase and that were a constant reminder of the viciousness and depravity that once he would not have imagined.

Tonight, though, tonight he could say to a friend, "It's all set now. You don't have to worry." It was late and he should have been tired, but Jerry Reardon felt like he could run a marathon or scale Everest. He had saved the daughter of friends. This job had always been hard. Lately, especially, as the possibility of retirement came closer, he had wearied of the legal system with its myriad loopholes and its "Let's make a deal" justice. "Burnt out" is an overused phrase. He wasn't burnt out. He knew that, but he was singed. That was for sure. He saw it in the morning mirror as he straightened his tie. He heard it in his voice, talking to his family and friends. He had become less patient with rookies, testier with colleagues and more likely to take a day off.

Every once in a while, though, there was a solid chunk of satisfaction. Tonight he had saved the life of a young girl. He couldn't think about Nancy and Louise. Tonight was about Molly. He knew that if he retired tomorrow, he would forever be the cop that "saved the Monaghan kid and caught the St. Anthony killer."

As he walked out the door of the police station, he spotted the deputy. "Take care" he said. "I'd keep a close eye on her, tonight." he advised.

"Sure. Thanks again. Be careful driving home. Those roads are treacherous." the deputy warned.

"Absolutely." He was used to the icy roads and usually dreaded long rides in winter. Tonight though he looked forward to the hours behind the wheel, which would give him time to think and to relax. First though, Jeremiah Reardon would tie up some loose ends and take some time to bask in the appreciation of a good friend. "Good work." he mumbled to himself.

A Sleeping Dog

Molly slept as she had not slept for a long time, perhaps as she had never slept nor would ever sleep again. She slept through the search of Polly Kuyper's house that revealed Nancy's scarf and other hard evidence against Kuyper. She slept right through Polly's stunning confession. Polly never articulated a motive for the murders. She would never give the police or the public the satisfaction of knowing why. Frankly, they didn't care. They had the self-confessed killer of Nancy Kiernan and Louise Porter. They had enough physical evidence to convict. They could close the book on those cases. There wouldn't even be a trial. Polly Kuyper managed to hang herself in her cell, the first night she was in custody. In the end what the papers touted was simply the story of a lonely spinster who had a history of mental illness and had gone so far off the deep end that she committed murder.

There was little sympathy for Polly. She had no family, no friends to mourn her. Ironically, like Louise, her death would be avoided in polite conversation. Because her death was so obviously a suicide, there was no funeral mass, nor was she buried in the University cemetery, as she had planned. It seemed that Polly had quite a bit of money, funds scrupulously saved and brilliantly invested. She left everything to the University. To their credit, they planned a memorial service for her sometime in the

Spring. She was an embarrassment to the University but a lucrative embarrassment.

Each day when the press came to visit, they were politely informed that Molly was sleeping and that she could not be disturbed. They thought it was a cover-up but Molly did in fact sleep through it all. She awoke on the third day, just as Father Tom walked into her room.

"I knew it." he laughed, "I knew Monaghan would rise on the third day."

She laughed, too, a real laugh. It had been so long since she could do that and then suddenly she wept Her body heaved with sobs. Every emotion, grief, fear, anger, love burst forth, torn from her at last. She cried for Nancy and for Tom and for Doc and Louise and even for Polly. Father Tom held her. "Go ahead." he murmured. "Let it out." Finally, she stopped. "I'm okay" She said. She put her hand on his shoulder. "I've drenched you."

"I'll throw it in the dryer. You've had a long sleep. Do you feel better?"

She wiped her face and blew her nose. "I don't know." she answered honestly. She touched the bandage on her neck. "I guess I'm okay. I have questions though."

"Of course, you do. You always have questions. Can they wait? Your mother's here and the boys are busy packing up your room. They need to see you."

"I need to see them. Will you come back later?"

"Certainly, you know I owe you a confession. This time we'll try the more traditional variety, where *I* get to grant the absolution."

Molly's mother swept into the room and held Molly close. At that moment, Molly realized that she had wanted her mother from that first day, that first morning she had seen Nancy's blood stain the snow. Just to be held safely in her mother's arms. Nothing could hurt her here. Here she was safe and warm and healed. Until now, she was afraid to yield to that, afraid once in her mother's arms, she would not have the courage to break that hold. Now, though it was a restorative. It was not a refuge.

Molly's mother told her, in no uncertain terms, that she was coming home. Mrs. Monaghan expected an argument, at least some protest. There was none. Molly was grateful. She wanted to go home, to sleep in her own bed, to hear the voices of her brothers, to catch up on the soaps and most of all to sleep, to have long nights of sweet dreams and late mornings.

EPILOGUE

The March morning threatened yet more snow. Students slushed along the crowded walkways, complaining about the cold, complaining about their classes, complaining about everyone complaining. Molly walked into the Arts building and shook the snow off herself with all the grace of a soaked St. Bernard. She went into Doc's office and left a folder on his desk. She scribbled a note on a slip of paper and left it on the folder. Then she went to say good-bye to Father Tom. To the surprise, even the shock of most people, the University had recently announced Father Benedict as the new University President. Tom Madden was leaving the University to teach for a year or two at St. Aidan Academy, a Catholic boys' prep school near New York City.

As she headed toward the Friary she was surprised to see Kevin talking with Father Tom in the doorway. They were deep in conversation and she almost apologized for interrupting them. Kevin had given Tom a bottle of Scotch as a going-away-gift. Molly hadn't brought a gift. She had talked to both Kevin and Tom on the phone, but she hadn't seen them since she left campus after the attack.

Kevin hugged her. "I've missed you. he said.

"Hello stranger." Tom said as he gave her a long hug. "You look much better than when I last saw you."

"You look great." She replied. It was an honest assessment. He looked younger and somehow happier than she had ever seen him.

Kevin suggested, "Why don't you guys talk for a little? I need to pick up something over at the yearbook office. Don't leave before I get back, okay?

"Have you made a decision about graduation? Tom asked. Molly was not graduating. She had completed her incomplete first semester courses, but she had withdrawn second semester. She debated coming to graduation, but she knew she couldn't watch Kevin walk across the stage. She had mailed her graduation garb back in February.

"I can't" she admitted and shrugged. She thought she could do this now. She could see Tom and Kevin and Clare and say goodbye and smile and it would be okay. She was wrong. She felt like she was unwinding.

Father Tom nodded. He had almost forgotten who Molly was. She was still a college senior who had survived the murder of her best friend, the knowledge that her mentors and models and friends were adulterers and liars and, thrown in for good measure, an attack on her life. Molly always seemed stronger, less vulnerable than she was. She hid her vulnerability behind wit and words. He knew though. He was her confessor and her friend. He had seen her in those early morning walks and in quiet times in the chapel and had dried his habit of the flood of her tears.

"I need to make a visit." He said. "Do you feel like keeping me company?

Molly nodded. Father Tom draped his arm around her shoulder. "Come along then."

They sat in the back of the Chapel.

"I'll miss this." Tom said quietly. "There's just something about this place. I've been in some of the most beautiful churches and chapels in the world, including the Sistine and somehow ... I don't know. I think this place is blessed."

"Me too." Molly agreed. "Well, not the Sistine, I haven't been to Rome. Someday maybe...I'm sure a Papal Invitation will arrive any day now. I think though this will always be my favorite sacred place. I'll miss it, too." Molly did not know when she would return, if ever. She tried to memorize the sight, to capture the feel of the place, to keep forever. Father Tom sat beside her. He was praying, almost silently. She couldn't hear exactly what he was saying, but the familiar cadence, his deep voice and the soothing rhythm of his words comforted her. After a few minutes, he stopped and looked at her, waiting for his cue.

"It was kind of a surprise, Father Benedict, I mean. I thought you were a shoe-in." Molly said quietly.

"I thought you'd be pleased."

Molly furrowed her brow. Was it possible that Father Tom didn't know how much she respected and cared for him? She didn't blame him for anything. Whatever he did or failed to do, that was between him and his God. Molly was afraid that she was the cause of his loss of the University presidency.

"Was it my fault?" she asked. She felt like a natural disaster that destroyed everything in her wake.

"Well, Molly, you had a lot to do with it. I like to think, though, that I was responsible. After you went home…after everything that happened, I had a long talk with the Abbott General. He sent me on an extended retreat. Don't make that face. It was the best decision of my life. "

"I kind of feel like I made a mess of everything and then ran away," Molly said sadly.

"You went home. You went home to think and to heal. I did the same thing. Neither of us ran away. Not this time. Speaking of not running away, I also had a discussion with the sheriff.

"That must have been bad."

"It was difficult, not bad. He thanked me for the background information, but said it didn't matter much. Ironic isn't it? We are all so self-centered. We think that the sins we carry around with us, the awful skeletons in our closet, will shake the world. Then, when we open them up to the world they barely cause a ripple. I'm glad I spoke to him, though. At least now they have a better understanding of Polly. You might not agree, but I figure she at least deserved that much."

"I do agree. I don't know why she killed Louise, but she didn't have to kill Nancy or try to kill me. In a million years, she seemed so harmless. Really, after her interview I was certain that thinking of her as a suspect was a sign of how off base we are, how ignorant and intolerant." Molly shrugged "I can't quite wrap my mind around any of this. It's surreal. I keep wondering if Nancy had picked something else or if I hadn't pursued it, I can't see that any good came out of any of it."

"I don't have anything to say to that. I don't know. If it helps at all, I can tell you what a friend of mine used to say, 'There are no accidents.

Everything happens for a reason.' He was this old monk, who had served in the missions in China during the Communist takeover. He was in prison and the Communists used to put arsenic in his food, not enough to kill him, just enough to destroy his digestive system. There were other things, too. He suffered. I used to marvel that he didn't seem angry about that, about the torture or the pain, the atrocities he had witnessed. That was his answer: 'There are no accidents. Everything happens for a reason.' So, I pass it onto you."

"The God's ultimate plan philosophy? I'm not a subscriber." She had heard it her whole life. It never made sense. She could believe the rest of it, no matter how incredible: the Virgin Birth, the Resurrection, even that the bread and wine she received in Communion was, for Molly, really the Body and Blood of Christ. That was doctrine of course, the plan business was just interpretation. Still, she couldn't count the number of those who espoused it.

"Maybe someday…." Tom suggested. "How are you doing these days in the faith department? Has all of this disillusioned you?

"A little, but it's not terminal. I'm not a fallen away Catholic. I may have stumbled a little." Molly confessed. "I've taken a little vacation from Sunday Mass." She found Mass unbearable. She kept thinking of that last Mass the day Nancy was killed and remembering Nancy's funeral, the white roses, the incense, the cold stark sorrow that shrouded the congregation.. She couldn't really talk about it. She smiled. "I figure I have some Mass credit, from attending daily here."

"You know it doesn't work that way." Father Tom said quietly. He knew. He read it in her face. There was too much down time in the Mass, too many meditational moments when it would be easy for feelings to surface. Molly would return. Until then she would pray and God would hear her prayers and she would remain in Father Tom's prayers and in his thoughts and in his heart.

"I know. I'll go back. Father, this will just take time." She was healing. Everyday Molly felt more rested. At first, she would awaken, frightened in the middle of the night. Those nights were infrequent now. She was at home and everything at home was familiar and comforting. She still could not sleep in the dark. Nights were tortuously long, but days were busy and exhausting.

Mornings the house was alive with the hurry-up of work and school. She would hear her brothers' voices, posing what seemed rhetorical questions "Has anybody seen my Bio book? Where's my gym bag? Their mother coaxing them to "put something in your stomach" Often there would be a knock on the door. "Moll, are you up? Could you drive me?" Sean would be holding the car keys. Sean was Molly's youngest brother and she adored him.

"I bet your mother is taking good care of you." Tom said.

"I'm totally ruined, but it's wearing off. You know Tess. I got a part-time job working in a bookstore. It isn't ambition. It's survival. Nobody can keep up with her. She's a mad woman." Molly laughed. "I get up to change the channel on the television and she says, 'While you're up you could take that laundry downstairs.' No wonder Daddy always worked two jobs. It was the only way to get any rest." Molly shook her head. "And it not just her, Sean decided that he's going to teach me basketball."

"Basketball? You don't seem the basketball type."

"Well, he used to play with Nancy when she stayed with us. I think he misses her."

"Nancy, really?"

"She was pretty good."

"I'm not surprised."

"I'm awful." Molly didn't run. She hadn't run since puberty. Before that, she had been a tomboy. She had played dodge ball and kickball and even touch football. She had climbed and jumped and run but she had never been fast and she would have life-long scars as testimony to her lack of dexterity. Her freshman year in high school, she had tried out for the basketball team, even though she had never played. Before tryouts the girls had to run laps around the gym. Winded and a lap behind everyone else, Molly opted out. That was when Molly changed from participant to fan.

To pacify Sean, she had gone with him to the gym to try again. After ten minutes she was afraid that her loving brother would succeed where Polly Kuyper hadn't..

"Again. Not surprised." Tom said. "I'll miss you, Miss Monaghan. I wonder who'll trade sarcastic remarks with me. Who'll keep me from 'believing my own press'? Wasn't that your phrase?"

"It sounds familiar. I'll miss you too, Father, but you're right. I am glad that you will be teaching and I bet Father Benedict will do a great job."

"You won't come back to finish up?" He asked.

"No, not now."

"I understand. I can send you my address when I'm settled, if you think you might write."

"I'd like that. Father, is it okay between us? Are we still friends?"

"We are more than friends and it is better than okay between you and me. Please know that. Wherever you go, whatever you do, I want you to carry that thought with you. Molly, I know you don't think much of God's plan theory but someday you might wonder a little about how Nancy and Kevin came into your life. You might conclude that your lives were intertwined and when that happened each of you became part of the other and that remains with you. I am grateful for all of you and especially for you, Miss Monaghan. I didn't suspect when I first saw you in my class how much you would teach me. Promise me that regardless of what happens you will remember that I pray for you every day and if you ever need me, you will get in touch. Deal?"

Molly stared past Tom. She couldn't look at him now. She didn't want to confront those eyes at this exact moment.

"Deal," she murmured.

They said a prayer together, and Father Tom blessed her a final time and went back to his packing. Molly waited for Kevin outside the Friary. Kevin asked about Tom and then said magnanimously, "I was wrong about him. He's quite a guy. I couldn't blame you if you were a little in love with him."

Molly whirled around. "I'm not a little in love with him, not that way, nor was I ever," she softened, "still I agree with you. He is quite a guy." Molly smiled, "Kevin, so are you."

"I knew that," he said, smiling "Do you think you'll ever come back here, Molly?"

"I don't know. I think I can finish somewhere else and just transfer the credit. There are too many memories. I'd drown."

"That makes sense. Here, the yearbooks came in last week and I got this for you." He handed her a bag with the yearbook. There was also a new St. Anthony sweatshirt. Molly looked away.

"Wow. This is hard," she admitted. "Thanks. You know, I need a new sweatshirt. I got the box with my clothes that you sent me, but I couldn't find my St. Anthony sweatshirt."

"I know." Kevin said ashamedly. "I still have it."

Molly laughed. "Did you bleach it or something?" Kevin had an assortment of clothes that were testimony to his lack of laundering skills.

"No. I just got used to you, I guess. So when it came time to send everything back, I thought it might be okay to keep your sweatshirt. Is that okay? It sounds a little creepy when I say it, but it seemed like a good idea at the time."

"I think it's kind of sweet." Molly said honestly.

"Sweet? I'm not sure I wouldn't rather have it be creepy."

"Okay, it's very creepy and it's fine with me."

" Molly, after graduation, I'm going home for the summer. Then I have plans to job hunt in New York but I'd like to stay in touch. I don't want to lose another friend."

"You won't, not even if you try."

"Are you all set? I'll walk you to the car." At the car Kevin kissed Molly and said a final goodbye. He watched as she drove away, then turned and waved at Father Tom, whom he noticed had been standing in the Friary doorway.

The secretary told Doctor Pascari that Molly Monaghan had visited and left something in his office. He was sorry that he missed her. He wondered if she had plans to return. Perhaps she had begun her thesis. That would be good news. He walked into the office and stared at the curious looking folder on his desk. The note read:

Dear Doc:

Enclosed you will find the investigative piece to complete the required course work for your class.

It was signed: Your shining light.

He picked up the folder and began to read. The work was entitled: *A Sleeping Dog*. It began: "*The rain broke through the heat. It hammered down upon ...*"

Made in the USA
Charleston, SC
18 October 2012